'Are you ...
want to ha ...

He frowned slightly. 'Why ...
you?'

She swallowed. 'For a joke?'

There was a long silence, and then he lifted a finger and touched her cheek gently.

'Someone did treat you badly, didn't they?' His blue eyes searched hers for a long moment. 'Well, just for the record, I don't make jokes like that. And, yes, I do really want to have dinner with you.'

'I'm going for a shower.' She determinedly turned on her heel.

'Fifteen minutes,' he called after her, his voice firm and very male. 'You have fifteen minutes to get ready or I'm taking you out as you are.'

She looked back, one eyebrow raised. 'Caveman tactics, Dr Macaulay?'

He grinned. 'Whatever it takes, Dr Weston. Whatever it takes.'

Sarah Morgan trained as a nurse and has since worked in a variety of health-related jobs. Married to a gorgeous businessman who still makes her knees knock, she spends most of her time trying to keep up with their two little boys but manages to sneak off occasionally to indulge her passion for writing romance. Sarah loves outdoor life and is an enthusiastic skier and walker. Whatever she is doing, her head is always full of new characters, and she is addicted to happy endings.

Recent titles by the same author:

THE PLAYBOY DOCTOR

BY

SARAH MORGAN

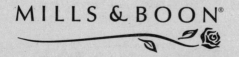

First published in Great Britain 2002
Harlequin Mills & Boon Limited,
Eton House, 18-24 Paradise Road, Richmond, Surrey TW9 1SR

© Sarah Morgan 2002

ISBN 0 263 83074 8

Set in Times Roman 10½ on 11½ pt.
03-0602-50305

Printed and bound in Spain
by Litografia Rosés, S.A., Barcelona

CHAPTER ONE

JOANNA WESTON pulled up outside a row of small, terraced cottages and switched off the car engine.

She felt exhausted. Totally and utterly exhausted. Her head was thumping and her eyes felt gritty from lack of sleep. Even blinking seemed to require a monumental effort.

To cap it all, she'd turned on the car radio in time to hear the weather forecaster cheerfully announce that it was the hottest June on record and the sun beating down relentlessly through the windows of her car just increased her drowsiness.

For a brief moment her eyes closed and she struggled against the overwhelming desire to sleep. She didn't have time to sleep. Not yet. Maybe tonight, if she was really lucky and everyone managed to stay healthy until the morning…

In the meantime, she had one more house call to make and then a busy evening surgery.

Forcing her aching, complaining body into action, she climbed out of the car and walked down the path towards the house at the end of the row.

The door opened before she'd had a chance to knock and she smiled at the old lady standing in the doorway.

'Hello, Alice. Sorry I'm a bit late. I had more calls than usual. How's that chest of yours?'

'It's much better.' Alice James stood to one side to let Joanna in, gesturing towards the kitchen. 'The kettle's just boiled and you look as though you're in need of some sustenance. Come and sit down.'

Sit down?

It was tempting, but Joanna had a suspicion that if she sat down she might never get up again.

'I shouldn't really.' She glanced at her watch doubtfully. 'Surgery starts in half an hour and I don't want to be late.'

Alice ignored her and spooned tea into a large blue teapot. 'The people in this village will be more than happy to wait an extra five minutes. We all know that you're working far too hard at the moment. I gather you were up half the night with Ted Rawlings...'

Joanna looked at her in astonishment as she put her bag down by the table. 'How did you know that?'

'I heard it from Doris in the newsagent.' Alice added boiling water to the tea. 'And *she* heard it from Geoff Forrest, the postman, whose mother lives next door to Ted and saw the ambulance in the night.'

Joanna gaped at her, temporarily speechless. She'd lived in this small, rural community for three years now and she was still surprised by the speed with which news travelled.

'Is *anything* ever private around here?'

'Not much.' Alice put the teapot in the middle of the scrubbed kitchen table and reached for two bone china cups. 'And you should be thankful for that. It was Geoff's mother who called you because she heard Ted moaning through the wall and was worried. If she hadn't, goodness knows what might have happened. So how is he now?'

'You mean to tell me that the jungle drums haven't given you the answer to that one yet?' Joanna's tone was dry. 'You know I can't discuss other patients with you, Alice. I'm probably the only person in the village who can't.' She reached into her bag and pulled out a stethoscope. 'Now, stop gossiping and let me listen to that chest of yours.'

Alice unbuttoned her blouse and made a tutting noise. 'You're not in London now, young lady. This is rural Devon, remember? It's not about gossiping. It's about being neighbourly. We all know everyone else's business here. You've been around long enough to know that. If you won't tell me what's going on then there's other folks that will.'

'I'm sure they will, Alice,' Joanna said calmly, placing her stethoscope on the woman's chest, 'so there's no need for you to put me on the spot. Anyway, I don't know why you're asking me. I seem to know less than anyone around here. I'm only the doctor. Deep breath in for me…and again… Great. Now, your back…'

She examined the old lady carefully and then unhooked the stethoscope and tucked it back into her bag. 'Well, that sounds a lot healthier than last time. Your chest is clear.'

'And about time! I seem to have been coughing for the whole winter and most of the spring, too.' Alice buttoned up her blouse and poured the tea.

Joanna looked at the steaming cup longingly and wrestled with her conscience. 'I haven't really got time for this, Alice…'

'Nonsense. You need a break after the week you've had,' Alice said briskly. 'Doris and I were talking about it only yesterday, and according to our calculations you haven't had an undisturbed night's sleep for two weeks! On Monday it was poor old Chris Rogers, then on Tuesday you were up with the little Blake twins, on Wednesday you—'

'Are you having me followed?' Joanna sank onto one of the kitchen chairs and started to laugh. 'You and Doris know more about my life than I do! If I ever forget where I'm meant to be, I'll give you a ring.'

'You may laugh, but that's what a community is all about,' Alice said firmly, opening a large cake tin and picking up a knife. 'Keeping an eye out for each other. Talking of which, we're all terribly worried about Paula and Nick since the accident.'

'Accident?' Joanna stared at her. 'What accident?'

Alice sighed. 'That precious little dog of theirs was killed on the road yesterday. He slipped his lead apparently and there was nothing Paula could do.'

'Oh, no.' Joanna felt a rush of sadness. She knew just how much that dog had meant to Paula. 'Alice, that's awful news.'

'Yes.' Alice nodded agreement and lifted the cake out of the tin. 'They adored that dog.'

'I know,' Joanna said gruffly, making a mental note to call on the family to check on them. She knew that they'd be feeling totally bereft.

'Anyway, enough of our problems,' Alice said briskly, pushing Joanna's cup towards her to remind her to drink it. 'It's you we're all worried about.'

'Me?' Joanna looked startled, and Alice nodded.

'Yes, you. Doris and I have decided that it's time we all looked out for you a bit more. You've been working all hours since Dr Mills went off to Australia, leaving you to cope on your own. You look shattered, pet.'

'Well, I am a bit tired,' Joanna admitted, giving a wry smile as she listened to herself. *A bit tired?* That had to classify as the understatement of the year! The truth was that she felt so weary she could barely stay upright...

Alice cut two large wedges of chocolate cake and passed Joanna a slice. 'You're overworked, Dr Weston, and we all know it. There are too many patients here for one doctor. It isn't right that you've been left to cope on your own. Dr Mills is the senior partner. He had a responsibility to check that you were all right before he took himself off.'

'Alice, I can't possibly eat all that,' Joanna protested weakly as she stared at the huge piece of cake in front of her. 'I'll pop. And Dr Mills didn't just take himself off—he arranged a locum to cover while he visited his son in Australia. He didn't know there was going to be an emer-

gency and that he'd end up staying. He only booked the
locum for two weeks because he only planned to stay that
long.'

And a total waste of space that locum had been, too!
Alice obviously agreed if her derisive snort was anything
to go by.

'*Him?*' Alice's mouth tightened disapprovingly. 'If he'd
spent less time on the beach, surfing, and more time doing
surgeries, you might have lost those dark circles around
your eyes.'

Joanna didn't even bother trying to defend him. Alice
was right. The man had been almost useless.

'Yes, well, he's gone now.' She took a bite of cake and
gave a moan of pleasure. 'Oh, Alice, this is sublime. You
must give me the recipe.'

'And when do you have time to cook?' Alice handed her
a cup of tea. 'Now you're without a locum, I shouldn't
think you have time to breathe, let alone cook. Are you
eating properly?'

Joanna smothered a grin, thinking that Alice sounded
more like her mother than her patient.

'Of course I'm eating properly,' she lied, pushing aside
a mental vision of her empty fridge at home. The truth was
she hadn't had time to think about food.

'Humph!' Alice's frown showed that she wasn't con-
vinced. 'Well, the first thing to do is get you some help.
Any sign of a replacement for Dr Wetsuit?'

Joanna laughed out loud at the nickname, knowing it was
well deserved. The locum had spent every available minute
surfing and had been next to useless as a temporary partner
in the practice.

'To answer your question, yes, I am getting a replacement. Dr Mills phoned me last night to tell me he'd found
another doctor to help me out until he can come home.'

Alice frowned and poured another cup of tea. 'And

when's that going to be? The man's worked in this practice for thirty years and he's never been away for more than a week at a time!'

'These are exceptional circumstances,' Joanna reminded her gently. 'His new grandchild arrived early. You can hardly expect him to come dashing home. His priority now is his son and their new baby. They need him.'

Joanna knew how worried the senior partner was about his new grandson. The last thing on his mind was returning to England.

'I know and I'm not blaming him.' Alice sighed. 'Poor Dr Mills. And poor Mrs Mills! Nancy must be terribly worried about it all. This was their dream trip—a visit to their son and his family in Australia. No one imagined that Melissa would have the baby early.'

'No, it was a terrible shock,' Joanna agreed, removing a cake crumb from her lap. 'But in a way it was a good job it happened while they were there. If Dr Mills hadn't been there, who would have looked after little Harry while his parents were at the hospital? He's only two, remember, and having the grandparents there has at least meant that Melissa and Sam can concentrate on the new baby without having to worry about him.'

'And how is the little scrap?' Alice sipped her tea. 'Any news?'

Joanna shook her head. 'Not since last week. But he wasn't too well last time I spoke to them. Twenty-seven weeks is very premature. He's got all sorts of problems, but hopefully he'll fight back.'

'Yes, well, if he's anything like his father he certainly will. Sam was always a plucky one,' Alice said, her eyes shining with memories. 'I remember him as a toddler, scrambling up the valley, playing in the river, running over the moor…' She gave a sniff. 'Crying shame they moved to Australia. It's too far away if you ask me.'

'He was offered a good job,' Joanna said, finishing her tea and glancing at her watch as she stood up.

'Humph! With a law firm? He should have been a doctor. Followed in his father's footsteps.' Alice stood up too and patted Joanna's arm. 'Mind you, then we wouldn't have had you as our doctor and that would have been a great pity. You're a very kind, very warm person, Dr Weston, and the best thing that has happened to this community for a long time.'

'Oh, Alice…' Joanna blushed and bit her lip, totally flustered by the praise. 'You're talking rubbish.'

'Not at all,' Alice said calmly. 'I'm just repeating what other folks are saying. Now, have some more cake.'

Joanna declined quickly. 'It was delicious but I couldn't possibly! I'll be the size of a house.'

'You? I don't think so somehow.' Alice squinted at her. 'You've got a lovely figure, dear, although if anything I'd say you've lost some weight lately.'

Courtesy of the empty fridge, Joanna thought wryly.

Impulsively she stooped to hug the old lady. 'Thank you for the tea and cake, Alice. I'll see you soon. Call me if you have any problems.'

She turned and walked towards the door and Alice followed her.

'So who is this new locum that Dr Mills has arranged? When is he starting?'

'He's meant to be arriving tonight,' Joanna told her, shifting her bag into her other hand as she reached to open the front door. 'As for who he is, I have no idea. I didn't ask. Dr Mills just said that he was a friend of the family and very well qualified.'

She didn't really care who he was as long as he didn't mind hard work.

Suddenly Alice looked interested. 'And he'll be living with you?'

'Well, not *with* me, Alice,' Joanna murmured, a trace of humour in her voice. 'But in the house, yes. Goodness knows, it's big enough. I'm rattling around in it on my own.'

And she hated it! Not that she'd ever admit that to anyone. An intelligent, adult woman wasn't supposed to have irrational fears, especially about something as foolish as being on her own in the dark. All the same, she'd lost count of the number of times she'd glanced nervously over her shoulder when she'd heard a creak, and she found herself double-checking the locks before she could sleep at night. Frankly she would be relieved to have someone else living there with her.

'Well, who knows, maybe he'll be handsome and eligible.' Alice's face suddenly brightened. 'You could do with a bit of romance in your life, Dr Weston.'

Romance? Hardly!

'I don't think so, Alice.' Joanna forced a smile, hoping it didn't look as false as it felt. 'Romance is the last thing on my mind at the moment.'

'Well, it shouldn't be.' Alice folded her arms across her chest and looked at her sternly. 'A young thing like you should be thinking of getting married and having babies...'

Babies.

Suddenly Joanna felt as though she'd been showered with cold water. It had been years, but it took so little to bring it all rushing back.

Once she'd hoped, *believed*...

But she'd been a gullible fool and she'd long ago resigned herself to the fact that she wasn't the sort of woman that men fell for. Marriage and babies were things that happened in dreams and to other people. Never to her.

Never.

Aware that Alice was looking at her curiously, Joanna

struggled to produce another smile. She didn't want the old lady guessing that anything was wrong.

'I don't care whether the locum is handsome or not,' she said briskly. 'I just want him to be a good doctor.'

'Let's hope he turns out to be better than the last chap,' Alice said, and Joanna gave a nod of agreement as she stepped out into the bright sunshine.

'Let's hope so indeed…'

By the time she arrived back at the surgery it was gone four o'clock and the waiting room was already full.

'I'm so sorry, everyone.' She gave them an apologetic look and shrugged out of her coat. 'I had more calls than usual so I'm running a little late.'

'Don't you worry, Dr Weston.' Doris Parker, who ran the newsagent, gave her a warm smile. 'We're happy just sitting here, catching up on the latest news, until you can get round to us.'

Joanna hid a smile, thinking how fond she was of them. Why would anyone want to work in an anonymous, faceless surgery in inner London when they could have this? It had its disadvantages, of course. Keeping a secret was impossible and everyone knew what everyone else was doing, but working in a semi-rural practice was so rewarding. This little village on the edge of Dartmoor was so much a community that you might have thought they'd invented the word…

Their kindness and understanding gave her a sudden burst of energy and she walked briskly through to her surgery and switched on her computer. She'd really try to keep the chat to the minimum, she told herself firmly as she called her first patient. It was the only way she stood a chance of getting through her list.

She worked her way through a steady stream of coughs, ear infections and rashes, and she'd just seen her last patient when Laura, her receptionist, popped her head round the door, her pretty face flushed with excitement.

'Dr Weston, look out of the window quickly—you have *got* to see this car that's just pulled into our car park.'

Joanna didn't glance up from her computer. 'I'm not that interested in cars, Laura.'

Especially not at the moment when she still had mountains of work to do.

'You'll be interested in this one,' Laura breathed. 'It's gorgeous. I've never seen one like it before. Except in the movies.'

Realising that the quickest way to be allowed to get on with her work was to look at the car, Joanna dutifully swivelled in her chair and adjusted the blinds so that she could see out of the window. A low, dark blue sports car had pulled in at the far end of the car park.

'Oh, yes. Very nice, Laura,' she murmured, wondering what it was about cars that got people so excited. For her they were just a means of getting around. And not always a very reliable means!

Laura walked across the room and stood next to her, peeping through the blinds like a naughty child.

'*Nice?* You think the car is *nice*? Dr Weston, that car cost a fortune. It's a—'

'I really don't care what sort of car it is,' Joanna admitted, interrupting her receptionist in mid-flow. 'A car is just a car as far as I'm concerned.'

'Well, that may be true normally,' Laura muttered faintly, 'but that's not any old car, it's a—'

'Laura, I'm really very busy,' Joanna hinted tactfully, watching with half an eye as the door opened and the driver stepped out of the car. He flexed broad, muscular shoulders and stood for a moment, taking in the surrounding scenery.

'Oh, wow!' Laura gave a squeak. 'Look at that body! The driver's as gorgeous as the car.'

Was he? Trying to hide her total lack of interest, Joanna stared at the stranger and wondered why she never felt the things other women seemed to feel when she looked at men. Was he gorgeous? He was too far away for her to be able to see his features clearly, but even distance couldn't conceal his powerful physique and the slightly arrogant tilt of his dark head as he stared at the sunlit moor. Then he turned, and in one smooth movement he reached into the car and retrieved a black leather jacket. Locking the car with a casual flick of his wrist, he slung the jacket over his shoulders and strolled across the car park towards the surgery.

'Pinch me.' Laura sighed, her expression dreamy. 'Pinch me quickly. No one looks like that in real life. At least, not on Dartmoor.'

Totally unaffected by what she'd seen, Joanna turned back to her computer, itching to get on with her work. 'You shouldn't talk that way about a patient, Laura.'

Laura looked at her as if she'd suddenly grown horns. 'A patient? He can't possibly be a patient. You can tell that man has never had a day's ill health in his life just by looking at him.' She glanced out of the window again and gave an audible gasp. 'Oh, Dr Weston, look at him close up! He looks like a film star. I'd better go and see what he wants. He's probably just lost and needs directions.' She straightened and hurried towards the door, pausing to throw a saucy wink in Joanna's direction. 'I may be some time. If he needs to know the way to paradise, I'll have to show him personally.'

Joanna shook her head with a smile as the receptionist left, relieved to be allowed to get on with her work. She was too busy to waste time gazing at strange men, even if they were supposedly handsome. Anyway, handsome men were bad news.

She was totally immersed in a stack of results when there

was a tap on the door and Laura entered again with a flourish, her cheeks slightly pink.

'Dr Weston, there's someone to see you.' Excitement mingled with admiration in her voice. 'A Dr Macaulay.'

Macaulay?

She looked up and blinked twice, just to make sure she was seeing straight.

Dr Macaulay. Sebastian Macaulay.

Here.

In her surgery. Lounging with careless arrogance against the doorway as if he owned the place. Which was entirely possible, she thought with a touch of irony. If memory served her right, the Macaulay family owned half of Britain. Which explained the flashy car in the car park, of course.

The question was, what was he doing here? The last thing she'd heard, he'd been spending his time jetting between Caribbean islands and other exotic locations. She couldn't imagine for a moment that rural Devon was on his list of desirable places to visit.

As their eyes met she saw recognition flicker in those blue depths and she braced herself for his reaction.

'Well, well, it's Joanna Weston…' His voice was a soft, cultured drawl and Joanna glanced quickly at Laura, her face expressionless.

'Thank you, Laura. I'll call you if I need you.'

Whatever derogatory comment Sebastian Macaulay was about to make about her, she didn't want him doing it in front of Laura.

Laura hovered, clearly wanting to stay around. 'Shall I get you some—?'

'I'll call you,' Joanna snapped, and Laura gave her a puzzled look, clearly taken aback that her normally mild-mannered, kind boss was behaving so uncharacteristically.

Joanna sighed, feeling instantly guilty. It wasn't Laura's fault. 'Thank you, Laura. If we need you, we'll buzz.'

Laura stared at her for a moment before turning and leaving the room, closing the door firmly behind her.

Sebastian Macaulay...

For a moment Joanna just stared at him and then she pulled herself together.

'Well, this is a surprise.'

'It is indeed.' His blue eyes sparked with wry humour. 'Although I suppose I should have guessed that it would be you. When I was told that this place was being run single-handed by a female GP, I was intrigued as to what sort of woman would want to bury themselves in the middle of nowhere.'

Nowhere? Joanna felt herself bristle. He thought this was *nowhere*? Well, someone like him probably would of course. She counted to ten and forced herself to be civil. She was *not* going to let the man wind her up.

She lifted her chin and gave him a cool look. 'I'm not buried, Dr Macaulay, and I choose to live and work here because the people are lovely and the countryside and the beaches are wonderful. Although this might surprise you, I consider this village to be *somewhere*, rather than *nowhere*. But I can understand how someone of your...' she paused for emphasis '...*sophisticated* tastes might consider this to be nowhere. Which leads us to the question of what you could possibly be doing in this area.'

Instead of answering immediately, he strolled round her consulting room, pausing to examine pictures, posters and photographs.

Personal photographs!

She felt a flash of anger and forced herself to calm down and analyse her feelings.

What on earth was the matter with her? How could someone she hadn't seen for at least six years provoke such hostility in her? She was confused and puzzled by her own reaction. She didn't normally respond that way to people. Normally she was placid and gentle, a real peacemaker. But Sebastian Macaulay had always brought out aspects of her character that she had trouble identifying. Just being in the same room as him made her insides boil and churn.

It was just because they were so different, she reasoned. Not just in terms of background—although that too, of course, because she knew for a fact that Seb Macaulay was wealthier than even Laura was probably imagining—but in terms of personality and attitude. How could she ever expect herself to have anything in common with a man who approached life as a game to be played and enjoyed, a man who shunned commitment and responsibility in favour of short-term pleasure?

No, she assured herself, her hostility towards him came from the simple fact that she disliked the man. She disliked the flippant way he approached life, the way people fell at his feet, his flashy lifestyle…

She bit her lip, forcing herself to face the truth. What she disliked most of all was the fact that he reminded her of—

Instantly she closed her eyes and pushed the thought away. She wasn't going to drag the past up now. Not twice in one day. First with Alice and now with Seb Macaulay. For years she'd managed to keep those hurtful, uncomfortable feelings totally buried. She was happy and she didn't want anyone or anything disturbing that.

Anyway was the man ever going to tell her what he was doing here? 'I'm very busy, Dr Macaulay.'

'So I hear.' There was a pause as he leaned closer to study a favourite of hers, a painting of the moor on a wild, winter day, and Joanna curled her fingers into her palms.

'Look.' She cleared her throat and kept her tone businesslike. 'Why don't you just tell me what I can do for you?'

He turned, subjecting her to the full force of his gaze. She stiffened, forcing herself not to react. She'd never met a man with eyes as blue as his. Just one flash of those killer eyes and women had fallen over themselves in their undignified haste to climb into his bed. Except her, of course.

'What you can do for me?' The corners of his firm mouth tilted slightly as if she'd just said something funny. 'It's more a question of what I can do for you.'

'What you—' She broke off, temporarily rendered speechless by his careless arrogance. 'Offhand I can't think of a single thing that you could possibly do for me except leave me in peace and allow me to get on with the mountain of work I have to do.'

His smile widened. 'That's the Joanna I remember,' he murmured softly. 'Work, work and then more work. Nice to know you haven't changed.'

His eyes left her face and wandered lazily over her body, starting with the flat, comfortable shoes, moving up past the sensible skirt, the crisply laundered blouse with the high neckline and finally resting on the severe hairstyle which she'd favoured since her second year at medical school.

She lifted her chin, his casual scrutiny making her hot and uncomfortable. She didn't need to see his slightly ironic blue gaze to know that he found her lacking as a woman. She knew that she wasn't his type. And she didn't care. She didn't want to be anybody's type.

'I'm very busy, Dr Macaulay.'

'So you keep saying. Which brings us back to the reason I'm here.' His tone was still amused as he walked over to the window by her desk and moved the blinds aside with one long finger. 'Nice views.'

'I'm not interested in what you think of the views. What has me being busy got to do with you being here?' Her tone was sharp and she frowned as he let the blinds drop and turned to face her.

'Rumour has it that you're in the middle of a crisis and you need a locum.' His eyes locked with hers. 'I know that you'll be delighted to hear that I'm that locum.'

She stared at him in stunned silence.

When she finally found her voice it cracked slightly, as if it had been kept in a dusty room for a month. 'You? You can't be my locum. There's been a misunderstanding,' she croaked, licking dry lips and rummaging round in her numbed brain for some sort of reasonable explanation. 'Dr George Mills, the senior partner, has made arrangements—'

'He has indeed.' Seb inclined his head in agreement. 'Me. He called me and I agreed to help out.'

'*You?*' Joanna shook her head slowly. 'No. That's not possible...'

He shrugged. 'Why not?'

'Because...because...' How could she put it without sounding horribly rude? 'Lots of reasons. You're not—I mean you don't— This isn't the sort of surgery for a man like you,' she finished lamely, wishing that he didn't always make her feel so tongue-tied.

'A man like me?' He threw back his head and laughed in genuine amusement. 'And you are such an expert on men, of course. Your specialist subject, if I recall.'

Joanna flushed at his none-too-subtle reminder that she'd barely socialised as a student.

'So go on.' He was still laughing, his eyes bright with humour. 'I'm intrigued to hear your opinion. What sort of man am I, Dr Weston? Do tell me. This should be worth hearing.'

Joanna gritted her teeth. 'Certainly not the sort of man to settle down in the middle of *nowhere*. This is rural Devon, Dr Macaulay, not cosmopolitan London. There are no hot nightspots, no clubs or fancy restaurants, and the nearest we get to retail therapy is buying eggs from the local farm.'

He lifted an eyebrow. 'Damn.' He clicked his fingers in mock disappointment. 'If I'd known that, I never would have offered to help out.'

Joanna felt her temper rise at his flippancy. The temper she'd forgotten she even had until he'd walked into her consulting room. Five minutes. That was all it had taken. Five minutes with Sebastian Macaulay and already she wanted to commit grievous bodily harm.

'I'm glad we're agreed that this place would never suit you—'

'Agreed? Oh, come on, Joanna! Unless my memory is faulty, you and I have never agreed on a single thing since the day we first met,' he drawled, strolling back across her consulting room and staring at a poster on asthma management. 'And we're unlikely to start now. But whether we agree or not is irrelevant. I promised George I'd help out and that's what I'm going to do. If it reassures you at all, I'm sure I can struggle by without clothes shopping for a few months. I stocked up last time I was in London.'

Joanna stared at him in barely disguised horror. 'Are you serious?'

He gave a nod. 'Absolutely. My favourite designer had just launched his new collection.'

She gritted her teeth, aware that he was laughing at her. 'I wasn't referring to your wardrobe, Dr Macaulay, as you well know. I was talking about the ridiculous suggestion that you should work here.'

'Why ridiculous?' He shrugged his broad shoulders. 'I'm as well qualified as you, and you know it.'

She was unable to argue with that fact. The truth was that, despite his casual attitude, Seb Macaulay was clever. Very clever. Not that he used his brain, of course. He'd socialised his way through medical school and had man-

aged to pass his exams having barely attended a single lec-
ture. In fact, he'd seemed bored with the whole thing. Until
they'd started the clinical section of their course. Once he'd
been allowed to see real patients, Seb had never missed a
day.

And since he'd qualified she hadn't heard much about
him. Just the odd rumour that he was doing glamorous jobs.
Which was nothing less than she would have expected. He
wasn't the sort of man to bury himself in a deprived, inner-
city practice.

Suddenly she was curious about just what he had been
doing last. 'So is that what you're doing at the moment?
Locum work?'

'Not really.' He suppressed a yawn. 'Actually, I've just
finished a stint on a cruise ship.'

Her mouth tightened. *A cruise ship.* Typical! 'I see.'

'I seriously doubt that you do.' For a brief second the
humour left those blue eyes and she caught a glimpse of a
side of him she'd never seen before. A serious side. But
then it was gone and he gave a careless shrug. 'But it
doesn't matter. George didn't stipulate that we had to understand each other—just that we had to work together.'

'We can't possibly work together, Dr Macaulay,' she
said stiffly. 'Our approach to life is too different.'

He gave a short laugh. 'Yes, well, fortunately we're not
talking about life here, we're just talking about the job.'

'You see?' She sat up straighter and glared at him. 'That
is *exactly* what I mean. To you it's just a job—'

'And to you it's your whole life,' Seb drawled, his eyes
narrowing as he watched her. 'Let's not waste time arguing
about which one of us is right. I seem to remember telling
you as a student that it was possible to work and have fun
at the same time.'

She was feeling totally out of her depth. She just couldn't
cope with someone like Seb Macaulay. He was too arro-

gant, too confident—too *male*. And he made her feel… feel…*strange*…

'Surely George must have known we'd have nothing in common,' she murmured, rubbing her fingers over her aching forehead. 'Why did he choose you? He said that he was asking a family friend—'

'I *am* a family friend.' He straightened and walked over to her desk, dropping his muscular length into the chair by her desk. 'I was at school with Sam.'

'Sam?' Her mouth fell open in disbelief. 'Sam went to the same school as *you*?'

Surely George and Nancy wouldn't have had the funds for that type of education for their son.

'Sam was a bright boy, he had a scholarship.' Seb ran a hand through his hair, his expression suddenly impatient. 'Look, enough questions. I thought you were supposed to be busy. If you've been handling George's patients as well as your own, there must be plenty for me to do.'

Offhand she couldn't think of a single thing. The mere thought of working alongside this man was so unlikely it was ludicrous.

'It won't work, Dr Macaulay,' she said finally, nervously touching a strand of pale blonde hair that had escaped from the knot on the back of her head. 'I'm sorry to have wasted your time but there's been a mistake. You'll have to find a job elsewhere.'

'Oh, for heaven's sake, Joanna!' He was visibly controlling his irritation. 'Look, I agree that this situation is hardly ideal for either of us. You think I'm a glamorous playboy with more money than sense, and I think you're an emotionally repressed workaholic whose idea of excitement is a night in with a textbook. It doesn't matter! No one says we have to like each other. We just have to work together and that should be easy enough.'

She stared at him, carefully hiding her dismay at his

words. Was that really how people saw her? *An emotionally repressed workaholic?*

'I can manage by myself,' she said finally, and he lifted an eyebrow in disbelief.

'With the number of patients you and George have on your lists? Don't be ridiculous. No doctor could manage that number single-handed. Especially in the holiday season. No.' He shook his head and gave a resigned shrug. 'You need help, and we'd better both just accept that I'm it.'

'Help?' Her voice rose and she almost winced as she heard herself. Normally she was a gentle, mild-mannered person and here she was acting like a fishwife. 'You're not my idea of help, Dr Macaulay—'

A muffled scream from Reception distracted her and Joanna broke off and tilted her head slightly. 'What on earth was that?'

Before Seb could answer, the door was yanked open and a breathless Laura stood in the doorway, her eyes wide with panic.

'Dr Weston, come quickly! Little Katy Ball has stopped breathing.'

Joanna stood up quickly. Too quickly. The room suddenly swam in front of her eyes and she swayed slightly. Immediately strong fingers clamped onto her shoulders and propelled her safely back into the chair.

'Are you all right?' Seb's sharp question penetrated the black fog descending on her brain and she nodded slowly, waiting for the dizziness to pass.

'I'm fine.'

'Well, you don't look fine.' His eyes were narrowed. 'You'd better stay here while I see to the child.'

'No!' Joanna stood up again, but this time more slowly, her fingers clutching the desk for support. 'She's my patient. I'll see her.'

'Well, join me when you're ready.'

The screams grew louder and with a last frowning glance in her direction Seb sprinted out into Reception, leaving her to follow at a slower pace.

'Dr Weston, help—help!!' Katy's mother was clutching the child against her chest, her face wild with fear. 'She can't breathe properly— Oh, God, please, help her, don't let her die. It was the bee, I know it was the bee. Oh, why didn't I see it?'

For a moment Joanna stood rooted to the spot, still feeling slightly odd, her mind totally blank.

Fortunately Seb's reactions were faster. 'I'm Dr Macaulay, Dr Weston's new partner. Give her to me.' He cut through Mrs Ball's hysterical rambling and swept the limp little figure into his arms. 'Laura, call an ambulance— tell them it's urgent. She needs adrenaline—fast!'

'In my room...' Finally Joanna sprang to life and she ran back to her consulting room, grabbing the necessary drugs.

'Why's her breathing so noisy?' Katy's mother had followed them and was hovering uncertainly in the doorway, her face chalk white.

'It's called stridor,' Seb said briefly, his eyes on Joanna as she drew up the injection. 'It's because her breathing tubes are swollen. Where did the bee sting her?'

'On the back of her neck,' Mrs Ball sobbed, 'it was such a sunny day I promised her we could have our tea in the park. The flowers are gorgeous at the moment. I didn't think about the bees...'

Seb held the child while Joanna gave the injection. 'We need to give her some oxygen and get a line in.'

Joanna nodded agreement and together they worked to stabilise the child. By the time the paramedics arrived, her condition had improved dramatically.

'I'll go with her in the ambulance,' Seb said briefly, and Joanna hesitated.

'I ought to go—'

'No.' Seb shook his head and helped himself to some equipment from her trolley. 'You're better off here in case someone calls you out. I don't know the area well enough. We'll talk later.'

And with that he strode after the paramedics, leaving her staring, open-mouthed, totally drained after the exaggerated emotions of the past few minutes.

She sank into her chair and stared blankly at the flickering computer screen.

How had this happened?

How had her neatly ordered life been turned upside down so quickly? One minute she'd been safe in her own little world, overworked but very happy with her daily routine. And then Seb Macaulay had strolled casually back into her life and triggered more emotion in five minutes than she'd imagined she was capable of feeling in a lifetime.

After just five minutes in his company she was ready to kill someone. And if he was intent on working as a locum, it was probably going to be him.

CHAPTER TWO

JOANNA was making herself some toast in the kitchen when she heard the heavy scrunch of ambulance tyres on the gravel. Wondering how on earth Seb had persuaded them to give him a lift back, she ran to the door, still worried about little Katy.

'How is she?'

'Fine.' Without waiting for an invitation, he strolled past her into the spacious hallway, a vision of self-assured, arrogant masculinity. 'They're keeping her in overnight for observation and then they're going to run some tests. She might need to carry adrenaline—that was a serious reaction.'

'It certainly was.' Joanna frowned as he hung his jacket on the coatstand in the hallway. 'What do you think you're doing?'

She'd been desperately hoping that he'd have changed his mind about working as a locum but, judging from the way he was making himself at home, it seemed there was little hope of that.

'We have things to discuss, Joanna.'

Deciding that there was no time like the present, she took a deep breath and looked him straight in the eye. 'Dr Macaulay, I'm very grateful that you helped with Katy but it doesn't change the fact that you and I working together is a ridiculous proposition. I'm sure now that you've had time to think about it you'll agree that it would never work.'

'It *will* work,' he said grimly, 'because it has to. I promised George Mills that I'd stay and help you until he comes

27

back, and that's what I intend to do. Katy's mother sent her thanks to you, by the way.'

Joanna felt a stab of conscience and bit her lip. 'It's you she should have been thanking, Dr Macaulay,' she said stiffly, knowing that it had been his quick thinking and actions that had bought them precious time. If he hadn't thrust her bodily back into her seat she would have ended up unconscious on the carpet. 'I apologise for earlier. I felt strange—I don't know what was the matter with me.'

His gaze was uncomfortably direct. 'You're exhausted, Joanna, that's what's the matter. How much sleep did you get last night?'

'Sleep?' She rubbed her temples with her fingers, trying to marshal her exhausted brain. 'I don't know. Not much. I was called out a lot.'

'Called out?' He frowned sharply. 'But you're on your own here. You can't be covering days *and* nights. Surely you're using one of the local co-operatives to cover the night calls?'

'George still likes us to do our own calls,' she muttered, her eyes sliding away from his as she braced herself for his reaction.

There was an ominous silence and when Seb finally spoke his voice rang with incredulity. 'Are you telling me that, as well as running this entire practice single-handed, you're *still doing all your own night calls*?'

'Well, I've been trying to.' For some reason the anger in his voice made her shiver. 'Since the last locum left it doesn't seem to be working—'

'I'm not surprised!' He gave her a look of total exasperation. 'No wonder your reaction times are slow. You must be comatose with exhaustion.'

Joanna was silent for a moment. 'I am tired,' she admitted finally, meeting that sharp blue gaze and then wishing she hadn't. There was something about Seb Macaulay that unsettled her. It always had. Even when they'd been students. He made her feel strange inside and she'd never been able to understand why.

He lifted an eyebrow. 'So why the hell are you being so stubborn? When are you going to acknowledge that you need help?'

'I have already acknowledged it, Dr Macaulay,' she said tartly, his tone of voice rousing her from her exhausted state, 'but you're not my idea of help. You're not what I need.'

'Not what you need?' He shot her an incredulous look and started to laugh. 'You, Joanna Weston, have absolutely no idea what you need.'

'Please, spare me your expertise in female psychology,' Joanna said shortly. 'I *do* know exactly what I need. A solid, sensible doctor who'll take his responsibilities seriously. You hardly fit that description.'

'I hardly think I'd want to,' he drawled lazily, an ironic smile touching the corners of his mouth. 'And if that's the sort of doctor you want to work with, I'd say you're in for a fairly boring summer.'

'I'm not looking for entertainment,' she reminded him. 'I'm looking for a colleague. Someone to share the work.'

'Ah, yes, work.' Seb leaned broad shoulders against the wall and surveyed her from under lowered lids. 'Your favourite companion. Tell me something, Jo, have you ever spent the night with anything more exciting than a textbook? Do you ever let your hair down—either literally or figuratively?'

'Not everyone approaches life in the same frivolous manner that you do, Dr Macaulay.' She gritted her teeth, hating the way he narrowed his eyes as he looked at her. It was as if he was trying to see straight into her soul. 'Work is very important to me, not that I expect someone like you to understand that. And *don't* call me Jo.'

'Oh, loosen up, will you?' He raked long fingers through his short dark hair, not even trying to hide his irritation with her. 'Work doesn't have to mean major self-sacrifice, you know.'

'Well, it certainly never is where you're concerned,' she replied acidly. 'Your last job was on a cruise ship. Hardly challenging medicine.'

'Actually, it was extremely challenging.' Suddenly Seb's eyes glittered ominously. 'A great deal more challenging than life as a GP in a community like this one.'

How on earth could pandering to the occupants of a cruise ship ever be considered challenging?

'Which just goes to prove that this isn't the sort of practice for a man like you.'

He straightened and moved towards her, his voice suddenly hard. 'What you know about me as a man—or what you know about any other man, come to that—wouldn't cover one page of a prescription pad. So don't prejudge me, Joanna. For the next few weeks, until George decides to come back, I'm your partner. Like it or not.'

A wave of exhaustion swamped her. Suddenly all she wanted was to go to bed and sleep. She didn't have the energy for any more verbal sparring.

'All right.' She took a deep breath, hardly able to believe that she was saying the words. 'If you're really prepared to bury yourself in the middle of ''nowhere'', and you're really prepared to pull your weight, I suppose I'd be foolish to refuse your offer.'

His smile was wry. 'Your overwhelming enthusiasm for my company is so flattering.'

Joanna's mouth tightened at his tone. 'Life's too short to play games, Dr Macaulay. I refuse to pretend to be pleased about something I know will never work. You know as well as I do that we've never seen eye to eye on anything—'

'Probably because I'm over six feet and you're barely

five feet five. Maybe you should try standing on a box when we talk—you might be more comfortable.'

She silently and slowly counted to ten. She'd always thought of herself as an incredibly patient person, but clearly she didn't know herself very well.

'This is never going to work,' she said heavily. 'You just never take life seriously.'

'Whereas you, on the other hand, take it much *too* seriously,' he rejoined, and she bit her lip, knowing that what he'd said was true.

She *did* take life seriously, but there were reasons for that. Good reasons. *Reasons he knew nothing about.*

She straightened her shoulders and looked him straight in the eye. 'If you're seriously planning to work here, you're going to have to accept the way I am, Dr Macaulay. Just as I'm going to have to accept the way you are.'

'The way I am?' He gave an incredulous laugh as he absorbed her words. 'You mean someone who enjoys life while he can—what's so wrong with that? Why is it wrong to approach life with optimism and humour?' He shook his head slightly as if he couldn't understand her attitude. 'There are so many awful things happening in the world that we need to grab happiness while we can. That's what I do, Joanna.'

'I'd noticed.' She couldn't keep the sarcasm out of her voice. 'And the chances of you and I working together for longer than a day without killing each other are so remote it's laughable. Now, if you'll leave me in peace, I was making myself some toast when you arrived.'

Joanna turned and walked briskly to the kitchen, hoping that he wouldn't follow her.

He did, and she gritted her teeth as he settled himself comfortably at the scrubbed pine table which dominated the room.

Seb's gaze followed her as she moved around the

kitchen. 'Is that all you're eating? Toast? Is there anything else on the menu?'

'Menu?' She glared at him. 'This isn't a restaurant, Dr Macaulay.'

Not only was the man content to torment her and totally disrupt her working life, he now expected her to feed him gourmet food. She took a deep breath as she removed the toast—now stone cold—from the toaster.

She knew she wasn't being very welcoming but she couldn't help it. The man drove her nuts!

'Look, let's start again, shall we?' Suddenly he looked tired as if he, too, was worn out by the tension between them. 'I've had a long journey and I'd appreciate some food until I can go shopping myself.'

He made her feel churlish and she blushed slightly, wondering what on earth had happened to her normal warm hospitality. Alice would have been horrified if she'd been present.

Admitting defeat, she gave a sigh. 'Please, feel free to help yourself to anything you can find, Dr Macaulay.'

As soon as the words left her mouth she wished she hadn't spoken. A man like Seb Macaulay wouldn't find much that would interest him in her fridge or cupboards.

'Oh, for heaven's sake, Joanna, when are you going to drop the formality and call me Seb?' Amusement vied with irritation as he got to his feet in a lithe movement. 'All this ''Dr'' business is a bit over the top, don't you think? We trained together. I've known you since you were plain Joanna Weston.'

And that was exactly was what she'd always been, of course. Plain Joanna Weston. Very plain.

She felt a shaft of pain and was suddenly hideously conscious of the crumpled skirt she'd been wearing since she'd been called out in the night and the fact that she hadn't brushed her hair all day.

'I like formality,' she said briskly, telling herself firmly that she didn't care what he thought. 'And the patients like it. It makes them feel secure.'

'Rubbish.' Seb was totally dismissive of her statement. 'People judge you on your actions and behaviour—not on your title.'

Refusing to be drawn, Joanna buttered her cold toast and took an unenthusiastic bite.

Seb watched her with an expression of disbelief. 'Is that seriously all you're eating?'

'I like toast,' she muttered, not bothering to add that she didn't have the energy to tackle anything else.

'Well, you at least ought to add some protein to it.' He strolled over to the fridge, jerking open the door to examine the contents. There was a long silence and then he glanced up, visibly stunned. 'Now I know why you're reduced to eating toast. Don't you ever shop?'

Joanna lifted her chin defensively. 'I haven't had time to shop, Dr Mac—Sebastian.'

Or change her clothes, or sleep…

'Seb.' He enunciated the word carefully, as if she were a toddler that he was teaching to talk. 'My name is Seb. For goodness' sake, practise it a few times until it feels comfortable.' He peered back into the fridge. 'What on earth have you been eating all week? There's nothing in here.' He reached into the fridge and pulled out a small piece of cheese covered in mould, which he looked at with distaste. 'For crying out loud, Jo, there's more bacteria in your fridge than in a path lab.'

'I don't like cheese.' She glared at him. 'And I've asked you before not to call me Jo.'

He ignored her, still staring into the fridge as though he expected to catch some hideous disease. 'What did you have for lunch?'

'Sorry?'

'Lunch.' He looked at her as though she were an alien from another planet. 'You know, the food that we generally consume in the middle of the day to give us the energy to carry on with our lives. What did you have?'

Joanna looked at him blankly, wondering why her eating habits were of such interest to him. 'I don't know. I— Nothing.'

Suddenly he was still. 'You didn't eat lunch?'

'I was busy.'

His breath hissed through his teeth. 'You're a doctor, Joanna. You should know better. How do you expect to be able to carry your workload without fuel? No wonder you nearly fainted earlier.'

'I didn't nearly faint—I just got up too quickly.'

'Right.' The disparaging look he gave her told her that he didn't believe her. 'What did you have for breakfast?'

'I was at the hospital.'

'For God's sake, woman!' He slammed the fridge shut and ran a hand through his dark hair, his expression exasperated. 'When *did* you last eat?'

'I'm eating now,' she said pointedly, taking another bite out of her toast.

'I mean proper food,' he growled. 'That's no good for you at all.'

Shaking his head with disbelief, he turned on his heel and strode back through to the hall, delving into his jacket pocket for his car keys.

'Where are you going?' She followed him, torn between outrage that he'd been so blunt and a faint hope that he'd decided he couldn't possibly work with her and was leaving her in peace.

'Shopping.' He shrugged his broad shoulders into his jacket and turned to face her, his expression ominous. 'You're almost burnt out, Joanna. You're starving hungry and exhausted, and unless you do something about it fast

you're going to collapse. Go and have a relaxing bath—
that's if you know what the word "relaxing" means, which
I seriously doubt—and I'll go out and buy us both something decent for supper. Something that isn't covered in
mould or hairs and isn't at least two months past its sell-
by date.'

With that he yanked open the door and crunched across
the drive to his sports car without a backward glance.

Fate was definitely not smiling on him.

Seb opened the boot of the car, removed the shopping
bags and glanced at the house.

Joanna Weston. Who would have thought it?

Of all the women in the world he had to be marooned
with, it had to be Joanna Weston. The irony of it nearly
made him laugh. When George Mills had rung him and
asked for his help, he'd anticipated a few months of peace
and quiet in Devon. A complete contrast to his normal life.
To be honest, he'd been pleased at the offer. The past year
had been particularly hectic and traumatic, and he'd been
looking forward to leading the fairly normal existence of a
GP in a semi-rural practice. When he'd heard how small
the community was and how isolated the house, he'd been
imagining it as his desert island. Somewhere he could relax.

He walked up to the house and pressed the doorbell. The
trouble was, Joanna Weston was most definitely not his
idea of a desert-island woman. Being marooned with her
was likely to be an extremely irritating and uncomfortable
experience. The woman didn't know the meaning of the
word 'fun'.

It was strange really, he mused as he waited for her to
answer the door. Normally he got on well with women. In
fact, it was keeping them at a distance that was usually the
problem. But that had never been the case with Joanna. She
was one of the few women he'd ever met who was totally

uninterested in him as a man. Actually, she seemed totally uninterested in any man. Since the day he'd met her at medical school she'd had her nose buried in a book.

He gave a wry smile and rang the bell again. Maybe he should look on the bright side. At least he didn't have to be on his guard with her. Normally he was very careful in his interaction with women, very careful to avoid misunderstandings. But at least with Joanna he could relax. There was absolutely no chance at all that she would ever fall for him. Which was actually rather refreshing.

Realising that she had no intention of letting him in, he gritted his teeth and stepped back, glancing up at the windows.

Was she playing games again or was she in the bath? Or maybe she'd already fallen asleep? The woman had looked totally wiped out, which was hardly surprising considering her lifestyle. Joanna Weston was a workaholic.

With a muttered curse he dumped the shopping on the gravel and strode round to the side of the house, looking for another entrance.

'Sebastian?'

Hearing his name, he turned and crunched back along the gravel to the front door. Joanna was hovering awkwardly, dressed only in a long white dressing-gown, her hair wrapped in a towel. Obviously she'd just stepped out of the bath and she looked strangely vulnerable, clutching the dressing-gown in her small fist, the dark shadows of tiredness under her eyes accentuated by the pallor of her skin.

She looked different and he frowned slightly, trying to work out why. Her eyes. Blue. Deep blue. Almost violet. Like a Caribbean sea on a bright summer's day. Why hadn't he ever noticed that before?

Because, he reflected thoughtfully, he was normally so

busy being irritated by her that he never gave a thought to how she looked.

'I'm sorry. I forgot to give you a key.'

Suddenly she seemed aware of his scrutiny and took a step backwards, clutching the dressing-gown as if she was afraid he might drag it away from her.

Seb almost laughed at the mere thought. It took more than a pretty pair of eyes to bring out the animal in him. Despite what many people thought, he was extremely choosy about his female companions.

'I've bought us some supper.'

Without giving her time to argue, he strode past her into the hallway and made straight for the kitchen.

He hauled the shopping onto the table and started unloading the contents of the overstuffed bags into the cupboards and the fridge, still staggered by how empty they were. What had the woman been living on?

Turning his attention to supper, he quickly stir-fried some chicken with fresh ginger and garlic and added some vegetables and noodles.

'I didn't know you could cook.'

She'd swapped the dressing-gown for a blue T-shirt and an old pair of faded jeans that clung lovingly to her slim thighs. Until that moment he'd never actually noticed her body before, but he saw now that she was tiny—more delicate than he'd realised.

Pulling himself together, he lifted the pan off the cooker and served the contents onto two plates then watched in amazement at the speed with which she devoured her portion.

She might be slight in build but there was absolutely nothing wrong with her appetite.

'Do you want some more?' He couldn't keep the amusement out of his voice and she raised her small chin defensively.

'I was hungry. And it was delicious.'

'Then eat—I suspect you're catching up on a week's worth of food,' he said gruffly, standing up and heaping another large helping onto her plate. 'The fridge is now full so there's no excuse for you to faint in my arms again.'

She glared at him, her fork frozen in mid-air. 'I didn't faint in your arms—'

'Joanna you're exhausted,' he said flatly, 'and it's hardly surprising. You've been carrying the workload of two GPs, and on top of that you obviously haven't been eating properly. You nearly fainted.'

Her eyes shot daggers at him and then suddenly her slim shoulders slumped. 'Maybe I did,' she mumbled, 'and I suppose I owe you a thank you. For shopping and for cooking.'

'Well, that's a first.' He leaned back in his chair, a smile playing around his mouth. 'Joanna Weston thanking me for something.'

'Yes, well, don't get too used to it,' she said awkwardly. 'I haven't slept properly for four nights. I'm not myself.'

He could see that she hadn't slept. She looked exhausted. *And pretty.*

He shook himself slightly. Joanna Weston was definitely pretty. Why hadn't he ever seen it before?

Because normally she hid herself behind drab clothes. Suddenly he was intrigued. Maybe there was more to her than he'd thought...

Seeing her almost dropping off at the table, he cursed under his breath. Joanna was totally exhausted.

'You ought to be in bed.' He stood up, the chair scraping on the kitchen floor. 'Just tell me where I'm meant to sleep and then you can go and get some rest.'

The drowsiness was gone in a flash and her blue eyes flew open. 'Where you're meant to sleep?' Her voice was a horrified squeak. 'I have no idea where you'll be sleeping, Dr Macaulay, but it isn't here.'

Dr Macaulay. So they were back to that.

He counted to ten—slowly.

'George told me I'd be staying at the surgery,' he said, emphasising his words carefully so that there could be no misunderstanding, 'and you know it makes sense. This place is enormous. There's plenty of room for two people to live together here and not see each other.'

She stared at him. 'Are you trying to tell me that you haven't sorted out any accommodation for yourself?'

'I didn't need to.' He tried hard to control his mounting irritation. 'When George asked me to help out it was on the understanding that I'd stay in the house. There was never any question of sorting out accommodation.''

A long silence followed and her gaze slid away from his. It was clear from her expression that she'd forgotten. 'Maybe that's true,' she conceded finally, 'but obviously I didn't know it was you.'

Seb ground his teeth. She might be prettier than he'd first thought but she was just as aggravating!

'Just point me to a room, Joanna,' he growled, his patience stretched to the limit. He'd never known a woman who could get under his skin like this one did! 'I'm staying here and that's final. And if you're worried about your virtue, don't be. I think we both know that there's no chance of either of us ever finding the other attractive. The best we can work towards is an amicable working relationship.'

The look of utter disbelief she shot in his direction left him in no doubt that she thought he was asking a great deal. It was obvious that she thought it extremely unlikely that they'd ever manage anything remotely approaching amicable.

And maybe she was right.

If there was a vulnerable side to her—and he was beginning to think he'd imagined it—then she kept it very well buried.

'All right,' she said finally, her expression grudging. 'You can stay, but a few house rules first.'

Seb closed his eyes and drew a deep breath. *Now what?*

'I'm a very private person, Dr Macau—I mean S-Seb.' She corrected herself quickly and paused slightly before continuing. 'I'd appreciate it if you would stay in your corner of the house and not come over into mine.'

What was she expecting? That he was going to jump on her in the night? She should be so lucky!!

'I'll try and remember that,' he said dryly, his humour returning as he suddenly realised just how much fun this could be. Every time he wandered into her side of the house she'd throw a wobbly. 'Any more rules I should know about?'

'I set the burglar alarm before I go to bed.' Suddenly her eyes slipped away from his. 'If you're out late, you'll have to turn it off and reset it when you come in.'

So she was nervous in this big house on her own. Well, well, she most definitely *did* have a vulnerable side.

'I'm sure I can manage that.'

'OK.' She ploughed on. 'About night calls…'

'We won't be doing any,' he said, smoothly interrupting her in mid-sentence, 'at least not for the time being. I've arranged out-of-hours cover for the next few weeks.'

She gave a gasp of outrage. 'How dare you? I don't—'

'You're exhausted, Joanna,' he said sharply, cutting through her protests before they'd really begun, 'and I don't know the area. Between us we're a liability. Once George comes back you can do what you like. Until then, we're taking whatever help we can get. Now, go to bed before you faint again.'

She shifted uncomfortably. 'I've already told you, I did *not* faint.'

He gave her a warning look. 'Either you go to bed voluntarily in the next ten seconds,' he said with exaggerated patience, 'or I'm going to carry you there.'

She stood up immediately, as he'd known she would. 'I'm going,' she said with quiet dignity, 'because I'm too tired to argue with you—'

'Alleluia,' he muttered, and she lifted her chin and walked to the door, glancing over her shoulder as she tugged it open.

'Don't think that the subject is closed. You had no right to change my arrangements for night calls without discussing it with me. This is my practice and from now on I make the decisions.'

With that she walked through the door and marched up the stairs, slamming what must have been her bedroom door firmly behind her.

The next morning Joanna stared at the packed waiting room in disbelief.

'Where have they all come from?' she asked Laura in horror. 'How can all these people suddenly have become ill overnight?'

'They're not ill,' Laura said with a giggle. 'They've just seen that incredible car in the car park and they've come to take a look at the owner! Talking of which, where is he?'

'I have no idea,' Joanna said shortly, picking up the post and flicking through it quickly. 'I'd assumed he'd be here to start surgery, but doubtless—'

'I *am* here.' Seb's deep voice came from behind her and she turned, her sharp retort dying on her lips as she met those cool blue eyes.

'Good. We're going to be busy,' she said stiffly, and he gave a careless shrug.

'I can cope with busy. I assume you just want me to see George's patients?'

'Yes—thank you. Laura will help you if you have any problems,' she said, and then gritted her teeth as she noticed the adoring look on Laura's face. Oh, for heaven's sake! What was it about the man that turned her entire sex into fools?

'Anything at all you need, Dr Macaulay,' Laura was saying breathlessly. '*Anything at all*, just give me a shout.'

Her meaning was crystal clear but Seb's response was suitably neutral.

'Thanks, Laura.'

Neutral or not, Joanna wasn't prepared to take any chances.

She nodded to Laura and then followed him through to his consulting room. 'Just one more thing, Seb.'

He settled himself at George's desk and flicked on the computer. 'What's that?'

Joanna steeled herself. 'Please, don't seduce my receptionist. Laura is very young and very impressionable. She couldn't possibly cope with a man like you.'

There was a long silence and then his eyes lifted to hers. 'A man like me.' His mouth twitched slightly. 'As I said last night, you know nothing about the sort of man I am.'

'I know that you're the sort of outwardly flashy, macho male that girls like Laura fantasise about.'

Just as she had about Charlie when she'd been Laura's age.

She almost laughed at her own thoughts. *Laura's age?* The truth was that she wasn't that much older than Laura was—she just felt it.

Joanna rubbed her aching temples with slim fingers. Goodness, she was tired. One undisturbed night didn't seem to have made any difference at all to the way she felt.

Seb's handsome face was expressionless and for once he didn't answer her.

She took a deep breath and tried again. 'I accept that you're not responsible for the fact that women throw themselves at you. I'm just asking you not to give her any encouragement.'

Finally he spoke. 'Did I give her any encouragement just now?'

She hesitated. 'No, but—'

'And I don't intend to,' he said quietly, leaning forward in his chair and returning his attention to his computer. 'Relax, Joanna. And don't worry about Laura. If it becomes a problem, I'll take care of it.'

Joanna licked dry lips. 'She's got a massive crush on you already.'

'Then I'll handle it,' he said calmly, his eyes flickering down the list of patients who'd booked to see him. 'It won't be the first time, trust me.'

She could well believe that. Women had always behaved really foolishly around Seb, and it was fairly easy to see why. He was rich and breathtakingly good-looking—qualities enough for most women.

But not her. She knew better.

'All right, then, I'll leave you to get on with your surgery. If you have any problems during your surgery, press the top right-hand button on the phone—it connects with my room.'

She gave Seb a brief nod and left the room, eager to get on with her own surgery.

Her first patient was Vera Peters, an eighty-two-year-old lady whom she saw from time to time with minor illnesses.

'Hello, Mrs Peters, have a seat.' She greeted the old lady warmly, wondering what the problem was. There were no clues in the notes. 'What can I do for you today?'

'My skin has flared up again,' Mrs Peters grumbled, 'It's really causing me problems.'

Joanna examined her carefully and gave a nod. 'I can give you some cream for that,' she said quickly, tapping away at the computer. After a few moments a prescription issued from the printer.

'Well, that was simple,' the old lady muttered, taking the prescription with a nod of thanks. 'I wish you could do something about my John as easily as that.'

'John? Your husband?' Joanna knew that the couple lived in one of the flats on the edge of the village. From what she knew, they seemed to manage very well. 'What's the matter with him, Mrs Peters?'

'He's stealing,' Vera Peters said crossly, clutching her handbag firmly on her lap and pursing her lips. 'That's what's wrong. He's stealing everything in sight.'

'Stealing?' Joanna looked at her in astonishment, surprised by the violence in the old lady's voice as much as by what she was saying. She'd always thought of her as a very gentle sort, the last person in the world to be aggressive. 'What's he stealing, Mrs Peters?'

'Things that aren't his.' Her fingers tightened on the handbag. 'Last week he took my handbag, this week it's my coat. I suppose he thought I wouldn't notice, with the weather being so hot, but he was wrong! I did notice.'

At least the man wasn't on the rampage in the local shops.

Joanna cleared her throat, trying to clarify what she'd just heard. 'So you're saying that your husband is stealing things *from you*?'

'Yes!' Vera glared at Joanna and then thumped her fist on the desk. 'And it's got to stop. And it's not just stealing. Sometimes he moves things just to annoy me.'

Sensing that the old woman was very upset, Joanna

reached across the table and gave her hand a squeeze, her voice gentle. 'What does he move, Mrs Peters?'

'My hairbrush and my shoes. They're never where I left them!'

'I see.' Joanna thought carefully, wondering exactly where the problem lay. 'And how is Mr Peters at the moment?'

'Same as ever. Difficult and cross. But he isn't ill, if that's what you mean.'

Joanna sat back in her chair and nodded slowly. 'Right. Well, don't worry too much about it at the moment, Mrs Peters. Let's give it a few weeks and see what happens. I'll need to see you again to check your skin anyway. We can talk about it again then.'

Maybe by then she'd have had a chance to question the husband.

She watched Vera Peters shuffle out of the room and made a mental note to visit the pair of them at home. Things often made more sense when viewed in the context of the patient's home life.

She called her next patient and worked her way steadily through to the end of the list, glancing at her watch in surprise when Seb strolled into her consulting room and announced that he'd finished.

'I thought it might be sensible if we did the calls together. I want to get a feel for the area. It's years since I was here.'

Joanna's heart sank. Have him in the car with her? She couldn't think of anything worse.

Before she could reply, her phone rang and she answered it quickly, her mouth tightening as she handed Seb the phone. 'It's for you. Someone called Gabby.'

'Gabby?' There was no mistaking the pleasure in his voice as he took the receiver and spoke warmly to the person on the other end.

Joanna was forced to listen as he made arrangements for that evening, irritation bubbling in her veins. It was so typical of Seb. He'd only been in Devon for five minutes and already he had women phoning him. No wonder he wasn't interested in Laura. The man probably didn't have time to fit her in.

He was going to be just as bad as Dr Wetsuit. Doing the bare minimum of work—

She stood up and reached for her bag and car keys, moving towards the door as he replaced the receiver.

'So...' His smooth voice came from behind her. 'Can I join you?'

What choice did she have?

'I suppose so.' She walked briskly through to Reception and nodded to Laura. 'We're off. If anything else comes in you can call me on my mobile.'

Seb adjusted his long stride to match hers as they walked to the car park. 'Do you want to take my car?'

She glanced at the long, low sports car and gave a wry smile. 'Not unless you fancy losing your suspension on a rutted farm track.'

To her surprise he returned the smile. 'Good point. It's not the most practical mode of transport for a country GP, is it? We'll take yours today, on the understanding that you let me take you for a ride in mine when we get back.'

She looked at him, startled. 'Why would I want to do that, Dr Macaulay?'

'For fun, Dr Weston,' he said softly, a strange light in his eyes. '*For fun.* You know, something you do simply for the pleasure of it. Haven't you ever done anything on impulse just because it felt right?'

For a brief moment Joanna stood frozen to the spot, her hands clenched on her car keys. The answer was, yes, she had. And she was still feeling the pain years later.

Shaking herself mentally, she glanced at him, flushing

under that sharp blue gaze. Bother. He'd noticed her reaction.

'So you *have* done something for sheer enjoyment—how interesting.' His voice was thoughtful as his eyes searched hers. 'What was it, Jo?'

'I've asked you before not to call me Jo.' She unlocked her car, anxious to escape from that narrowed gaze.

'Why?' Seb slid into the car next to her, fastened his seat belt and shifted slightly so that he could look at her. 'Did someone else call you that? Does it bring back memories?'

'No, it does not.' She gritted her teeth and started the engine, her stiff profile warning him not to ask any further questions. Over the years she'd tried to come to terms with her past and she didn't want to think about it more than she had to. And she most certainly didn't intend to discuss it with Seb Macaulay. 'And if you don't mind, I'd rather we confined our conversation to work from now on.'

'Why?' His eyes were suddenly curious. 'Why can't we have more general conversations? You never know. We might suddenly discover that we like each other.'

She gave him a withering look. 'I think we both know that there's very little chance of that, Dr Macaulay.'

It was bad enough working with him. She certainly didn't intend their relationship to get more personal than that. And as for actually *liking* him—well, she'd never heard anything so ridiculous in her whole life.

CHAPTER THREE

'So who are we visiting first?' Seb pulled the list out of
his bag and scanned it quickly. 'Ruth Kenton. Thirty weeks
pregnant. What's the history?'

Joanna turned the car onto a farm track and slowed her
speed as she carefully negotiated the potholes. 'The baby
isn't growing as it should and we're all monitoring her
really closely. She's got moderate pre-eclampsia, which is
probably affecting the growth of the baby.'

Seb lifted an eyebrow. 'Shouldn't she be in hospital?'

'Possibly.' Joanna nodded. 'But I'm working closely
with the consultant and we've agreed that she can stay at
home providing she rests and we check her daily.'

Seb frowned. 'That makes a heavy workload for you.'

Joanna shrugged. 'Helen, the community midwife, does
the lion's share. She's keeping a close check on Ruth's
weight and blood pressure, as well as her urine and the
foetal heart. The consultant started her on low-dose aspirin
a while ago,' she told him, pulling a face as the car lurched
into a pothole. 'Bother. This road is appalling.'

'It would be easier for you if she went into hospital.'

'Easier for me, yes, but not for her. This is a rural community,' Joanna said quietly, pulling up in front of a rambling farmhouse and switching off the engine. 'If Ruth goes
into hospital, it means that her husband will have to make
a sixty-mile round trip every time he wants to visit her, and
that's not practical. Like most farmers these days, he's
stretched to the limit.'

'So you're keeping her at home for his sake?'

'For everyone's sake. She's more relaxed in her own

home and she isn't worried about her husband travelling long distances to see her when he should be working on the farm. He's happy because she's under his nose. Anyway, she doesn't need to go into hospital yet. And when she does, we'll send her there.' Joanna opened the car door and smiled as four dogs surged round her, barking furiously. 'Hello, you gorgeous things.'

Joanna stooped to pat them, laughing with delight as they jumped all over her, their tails wagging. She realised that Seb was watching her with an odd expression on his face, and the laughter died in her throat.

'What?' She stiffened self-consciously. Why was he staring at her?

'That's the first time I've ever seen you laugh.' He took a step backwards as she stalked past him and lifted a hand to ring the doorbell.

'I laugh all the time,' she said frostily. 'I just don't laugh at the same things as you.'

'Obviously not. I didn't have you down as a dog sort of person.' He was looking at her with frank curiosity and she grew defensive.

'And what exactly does a "dog sort of person" look like?'

'I don't know.' His broad shoulders lifted and for once in his life he seemed to be struggling to find the right words. 'I just didn't think you—'

Before he could complete his sentence the door opened and a young woman with a neat pregnancy bump opened the door.

'Oh, hello, Dr Weston. Come on in.' She looked at Seb suspiciously and Joanna gave her a smile and introduced him.

'This is Dr Macaulay. He's my new partner, here to cover for Dr Mills until he's back from Australia.'

Ruth's gaze was suddenly hostile. 'Well, I hope you're

more use than the last doctor who came to supposedly *help* poor Dr Weston.'

Seb looked taken aback. 'Well, er, I certainly intend—'

'He was totally useless,' Ruth interrupted, standing aside so that they could both enter the house. 'Poor Dr Weston worked herself to the bone, covering for him. We were all glad when he left, weren't we, Dr Weston?'

'Well, he had his good points,' Joanna said, trying to be tactful as she followed Ruth through to the homely sitting room. The sun shone through the huge windows, illuminating the piles of magazines and cushions piled haphazardly on old, battered sofas.

Joanna put her bag down and sat down next to Ruth. 'So, how have you been?'

'Oh, fine,' Ruth said brightly, patting her stomach gently. 'But I must say that sitting around is pretty boring.'

Joanna examined Ruth's fingers for swelling and then looked at the rest of her body. 'You're a bit swollen, Ruth.'

A flash of panic crossed the young woman's face. 'The weather's hot, Dr Weston.'

'I know that.' Joanna removed a stethoscope from her bag and checked the woman's blood pressure.

'Is it high again?' Ruth chewed her lower lip as she waited for an answer.

Joanna hesitated. 'It's OK. Still up, obviously, but it's holding steady,' she said. 'We need to check it again tomorrow. Have you done me a urine sample?'

She tested the sample, recorded the results and then settled herself back down next to Ruth, who looked at her anxiously.

'I'm going to have to go into hospital, aren't I?'

Joanna shook her head. 'No. Not yet. But you know that the possibility is always there.'

Ruth nodded wordlessly and Joanna glanced at the notes.

'You're going on Friday for another scan—who's taking you?'

'Tom. He's got cover for the afternoon. Do you think they'll keep me in, Dr Weston?'

'I don't know,' Joanna said honestly. 'They might. It depends on the growth of the baby. You know that last time they scanned you they thought that part of the placenta wasn't functioning properly.'

'I know, and I'm really worried about it.' Ruth's voice was suddenly choked. 'Why me? Why me, Dr Weston? Other people have babies all the time with no problem at all. They pop them out as if it's the easiest thing in the world. But with me everything is going so wrong...'

She started to cry and Joanna slipped an arm round her shoulder and gave her a hug.

'Try not to upset yourself, Ruth,' she said softly, holding the young woman as she sobbed. 'I know it seems unfair, but it's best not to dwell on other people's pregnancies and birth if you can help it. Just focus on coping with what's happening to you.'

'But they said at the hospital that if he stops growing or my blood pressure goes up any more, they'll just have to deliver him—and he's only thirty weeks.' Ruth sniffed and wiped her eyes on her sleeve. 'He's going to die, I *know* he's going to die, and we've wanted a baby for so long—'

'He's not going to die, Ruth,' Joanna said firmly, 'That's why we're keeping such a close eye on you. They have fantastic facilities at the hospital. If he has to be delivered early, it's certainly true that he'll be very small and will have to stay in for quite a few weeks, but eventually you'll be able to bring him home safe and sound.'

'But how would we manage if he was in hospital all that time?' Ruth reached up her sleeve and pulled out a tissue. 'They said that he could be in for weeks and weeks, and I won't be able to drive because I'll need a Caesarean section. Tom can't do that journey every day—our business will go under. And I won't be able to see my baby.'

'Can I say something?' Seb's calm voice stopped Ruth's tears and she looked up in surprise, as if she'd forgotten he was there. 'It seems to me that you're worrying about too many things before they happen. At the moment the baby is still safely inside you, which is exactly where the hospital will keep him until they feel there's no other choice but to deliver him.'

'But he's definitely going to come early,' Ruth told him miserably, shredding a tissue with shaking fingers. 'And I don't know how we're going to manage.'

'The hospital should be able to provide accommodation for at least two weeks,' Joanna reassured her, 'and maybe longer than that. Dr Macaulay's right, Ruth. You're worrying too much about things that haven't happened yet, and it's not good for you.'

Ruth bit her lip. 'Well, that's all I've got to do, sitting here with my feet up, "resting". I've got too much time on my hands, that's the trouble. Too much time to think and worry.'

'I'll make some enquiries about accommodation,' Joanna said, giving Ruth's shoulders a squeeze before standing up and snapping her case shut. 'That way at least you'll know what the options are if you do have to go in early. In the meantime, let me know how you get on at the hospital on Friday.'

'I will, Dr Weston. And thanks. You're such a kind person.'

Joanna blushed, aware of Seb's scrutiny. 'Not at all,' she said briskly, 'Any doctor would have done the same.'

Ruth shook her head. 'No. Lots of doctors wouldn't bother, and don't think I don't know that. They would have left it to the midwife or had me admitted to hospital. You're the reason I'm still at home, Dr Weston, and Tom and I are really grateful for that.'

'You're very welcome,' Joanna said quietly, embarrassed by the praise.

Seb turned to her as they climbed back into the car. 'She's right, you know. Lots of doctors wouldn't have bothered doing what you're doing. They wouldn't want to take the risk and they wouldn't want to make life so hard for themselves. You've been good to her.'

Joanna frowned and turned the car carefully back towards the lane. 'Are you saying that you think I'm taking a risk with the baby's health?'

'No.' He shook his head and gave her a wry smile. 'Calm down. For once I'm not arguing with you. I don't think you're taking a risk because you're prepared to monitor her so closely. I'm just saying that the approach you're taking is making you a great deal of extra work.'

'Well, aside from the work, I actually think she's likely to do better, staying in her own home,' Joanna said, indicating right and turning onto the main road. 'Hospitals are notoriously stressful places at the best of times. I always think it's something of an irony that they admit pregnant women to hospital for rest.'

Seb laughed. 'You've probably got a point.' He glanced down at the list. 'Who's next?'

'Ian Clarkson,' Joanna told him. 'He's a fifty-five-year-old with chronic obstructive pulmonary disease. He's not on the list but he had a pretty awful winter, poor chap, and he's been trying desperately hard to give up smoking. He'll never come to the surgery unless he's at death's door, so I want to check up on him.'

She pulled up outside a row of cottages and walked briskly up the path to the front door of one of them, Seb keeping pace beside her.

The door opened immediately and an overweight, balding man greeted her with a smile. 'What a lovely surprise! Come on in, pet, I'm just about to put the kettle on.'

Joanna smiled and followed him into the house. 'Haven't really got time for tea today, Ian, but thanks anyway. I've got our new locum, Dr Macaulay, with me. I'm just showing him round.'

'Right.' Ian turned and stared at Seb and then gave a nod. 'And you've moved in with our Dr Weston, have you?'

Seb cleared his throat. 'Well, yes, in a manner of speaking.'

'Good.' Ian wheezed slightly as he filled the kettle and flicked the switch. 'That girl shouldn't be on her own in that big house. I've said it before and I'll say it again.' He turned and took another look at Seb. 'At least you're built like a proper man—should be able to cope with any intruders.'

'I'll do my best,' Seb said dryly, his eyes narrowing slightly as they rested on Joanna's tense features. 'Have you had intruders?'

'Just children,' she said quickly, avoiding his gaze. 'It happened just after Dr Mills left for Australia, so I suppose they knew I was on my own.'

'You shouldn't have been on your own,' Ian growled. 'There are too many things that could happen in a house that size. How's that roof of yours, by the way? Everything fine?'

'Brilliant.' Joanna gave him a grateful smile and then turned to Seb. 'Ian saved my life a few months ago. I had a leak in the middle of that awful wet spell and Ian sorted it out for me. He's a roofer. Anyway, enough of that. I popped in to find out how much you're smoking, Ian.'

'Haven't had one for three weeks,' Ian said proudly, and Joanna leaned forward and hugged him in delight.

'Ian, that's fantastic. I'm so proud of you.'

'Yes, well, there's no way I'm having another winter like the last one,' he said gruffly. 'I figure I've got the summer to get myself right. I've had terrible cravings, mind, but I rang that number you gave me and I joined that stop-smoking group in the village.'

'You're a total star, Ian! How much are you using your inhaler now?' Joanna asked.

He pulled a face. 'Varies. About three times a day, I suppose.'

'That's good. It's time I gave you a proper check-up so next time you're near the surgery get Laura to slot you in. Will you do that, Ian?'

'You're the boss.' He gave a smile. 'Are you sure you won't have a cup of tea?'

She shook her head. 'No, but thanks for the offer. I've got a list of calls as long as my arm to do.'

'Well, thanks for calling Doctor,' Ian said as he showed them to the door. 'And any problems with the surgery building while Dr Mills is away—don't be afraid to give me a ring. Anything at all.'

'Thanks, Ian.'

They said their farewells and climbed back into the car, working their way steadily down the list.

After their last call Joanna sat in the driver's seat, her expression thoughtful. 'I've got one more call to make,' she said quietly, 'but I'll drop you back at the surgery first.'

Seb frowned. 'Why?'

'Because it's a bit sensitive.'

'I'm a doctor, Joanna,' he said impatiently. 'I can deal with sensitive.'

She hesitated and then gave a little shrug. 'All right.'

Why not? He'd think she was mad, but who cared? His opinion of her was already so low it really didn't matter what he thought.

She pulled up outside a small terraced house and switched off the engine.

'So why are we here?' Seb undid his seat belt. 'Why is it sensitive?'

'Their dog was killed on the road yesterday,' Joanna muttered, not quite able to meet his eyes. 'I want to check up on them.'

There was a long silence while he digested her words. 'You're visiting them because they've lost their *dog*?'

The incredulous note in his voice made her lift her chin defensively. 'He was more than a dog to them,' she said shortly, 'and you can stay in the car if you like.'

With that she climbed out of the car and walked briskly down the path towards the front door.

A woman answered the door with eyes red-rimmed from crying. 'Oh, Dr Weston…'

'I heard from Alice,' Joanna said quietly, aware that Seb had joined her. 'I'm so sorry, Paula. I know how much you loved your dog. I just wanted to check that you were all right. I brought my new locum with me, Dr Macaulay. I hope you don't mind.'

Paula sniffed hard. 'He must think you're mad, doing a house call because someone's lost their dog. You must have a hundred more important things to do.'

'I haven't,' Joanna lied, ignoring Seb's incredulous glance. 'I'm having a very quiet afternoon and I wanted to see you.'

'Have you got time to come in?' The timid way she spoke indicated that Paula didn't hold out much hope, but Joanna nodded and smiled gently.

'Plenty of time. Any chance of a cup of tea?'

It was half an hour later—a half hour in which both she and Seb had been shown photos of the dog and had admired various rosettes—when Joanna finally stood up.

'Well, I'd better go. You and Nick are bound to feel very

down for a while, Paula, but if you're worried about how you're feeling pop in and see me.'

'Thanks, Dr Weston.' Paula walked to the door with them. 'I feel better, having talked to you.'

'Good.' Joanna reached out and gave the woman's shoulder a squeeze before walking briskly back to her car.

'I can't believe you did a house call because someone lost their dog,' Seb muttered finally as they drove back towards the surgery.

'To them it's as big a bereavement as losing a child,' Joanna said shortly, pulling up in the car park next to his sports car. She stared straight ahead of her, remembering the day Paula had dropped by the surgery to show her their new puppy. 'Paula and Nick tried for ten years to have a child and used up most of their savings on IVF that didn't work. By the time they'd resigned themselves to the fact that they were never going to have their own, they were told that they were too old to adopt. That dog was the child they never had. Not that I expect someone like you to understand that. Love and commitment aren't your strong points, are they, Dr Macaulay?'

She remembered from medical school that he'd had the reputation of never going out with the same woman twice.

For once Seb ignored the jibe, his mind obviously elsewhere. 'It's no wonder you're exhausted,' he said. 'It strikes me that you're carrying the emotional and physical welfare of this entire community single-handed.'

She shrugged. 'It's my job, Seb, and I love it.'

'I know you do.' He swivelled in his seat so that he could see her properly, his eyes scanning her face. 'And the patients love you back. And I have to admit that I'm stunned by the change in you when you're working. You're nothing like the person I thought you were at med school.'

She lifted an eyebrow. 'You mean I'm not an "ice maiden" after all?'

He had the grace to look slightly uncomfortable that she was aware of the nickname they'd given her, but the truth was she wasn't bothered by it. The nickname had never hurt her. If anything, it had helped to protect her from unwanted attention.

'But you're not, are you Joanna?' He looked at her thoughtfully. 'You're a completely different person with your patients. Do you realise that you hugged almost every single person you saw this morning—and there was me thinking you weren't tactile.' He shook his head slowly and then his eyes gleamed. 'What would it take to get you to hug me, I wonder?'

'Hug *you*?' She gaped at him, her expression incredulous. 'Why would I want to hug *you*?'

'Obviously you wouldn't,' he said dryly. 'Presumably because I'm a rampant, healthy male and not sick or wounded.'

She felt the colour flood into her cheeks. She didn't need reminding that he was a healthy male. 'I don't know what you mean.'

'Oh, yes, you do.' His voice was soft. 'You're quite happy to give all your warmth to your patients because sick people don't try and wriggle their way through that armour of yours, do they? Why are you hiding your true self, Joanna?'

'I'm not hiding anything, and you're talking nonsense,' she said quickly, fumbling with the doorhandle as she tried to make her escape. 'Come on. We've got work to do.'

'Work!' He leaned his head back against the seat and gave a low growl of frustration. 'Do you ever think of anything other than work?'

She opened her mouth to speak but he lifted a hand, obviously controlling his irritation with difficulty.

'All right, then, let's talk about work if that's what you want to do. We may as well agree how we're going to play the next few weeks. I arranged cover for the nights but not for every evening. I was thinking that we could work alternate evenings. That way we can each have time off.'

'I don't mind covering evenings,' she said, switching off the engine and reaching into the back seat for her bag. 'I'm sure you've got better things to do than hang around here, waiting for calls. Like seeing Gabby, for instance.'

His gaze was steady. 'Why would you mind if I see Gabby?'

'Mind?' She brushed a strand of blonde hair away from her face with impatient fingers. 'I don't mind what you do or who you see as long as it doesn't stop you pulling your weight.'

'So why do I detect a note of jealousy in your voice, Dr Weston?'

'Jealousy?' She slammed the car door shut. 'Don't be ridiculous. Why would I be jealous? I certainly don't want to spend the evenings with you. The days are going to be bad enough.'

'Ouch. And there was I congratulating myself on the fact that we'd managed to survive several hours together without bloodshed.' He broke off and took a deep breath. 'Look, I've got a suggestion…'

'What now?' Her eyes narrowed suspiciously and he sighed and raked long fingers through his dark hair.

'Like it or not, we seem to be colleagues—temporarily at least. So I think we should call a truce.'

Joanna stared at him. 'A truce?'

'Yes.' He shrugged his broad shoulders and gave her a funny, lopsided smile. 'We agree that I don't go on about the fact that you're a workaholic and you don't make sly digs about my supposedly frivolous lifestyle.'

A truce?

She nibbled her lower lip thoughtfully. It made sense… 'No arguing?'

'Absolutely no arguing,' he said firmly. 'What do you say?'

She was silent for a moment. 'All right,' she said slowly, her eyes wary as they lifted to his. 'We'll give it a try.'

'Good.' Seb immediately held out his hand and she gave him hers reluctantly, trying not to notice the strength and power in those fingers as they closed over hers.

Would it work? She had a feeling that it would take more than a truce for them to live and work together amicably. Only time would tell…

The next morning Joanna awoke early, immediately aware of the sun shining through a gap in the curtains. A glance at the clock told her that it was only five o'clock. Instead of going back to sleep, she slid out of bed and padded to the window, a soft smile touching her face as she saw her horse, Romeo, grazing in the paddock at the bottom of the garden. She hadn't been to see him since Seb had arrived. She hadn't wanted her new colleague to see the other side of her. She still didn't. Truce or not, she had no intention of revealing more of herself than she had to.

Suddenly her eyes narrowed and she glanced at her watch again.

Why not?

No one else would be awake at this hour…

Her decision made, she turned and yanked open her wardrobe, removing a pair of cream jodhpurs. She dressed in seconds, slipping her feet into ankle boots and not even bothering to remove the thin T-shirt she wore to bed. Despite the hour, it was already warm outside. She'd be fine as she was.

Her hair fell in tumbled waves over her shoulders but for once she ignored it, cramming a hard hat onto her head and running nimbly down the stairs.

She let herself quietly out of the back door, whistling softly to the large horse who trotted over to the gate.

Not bothering with a saddle or a bridle, she attached a rope to his head collar and sprang easily onto his back, loving the feel of his familiar warm flesh against her body. She loved riding bareback. It made her feel part of the horse.

She rubbed a hand down his neck and dropped a kiss on his mane.

'I need to let off steam, Romeo. I hope you do, too.' She made a soft clicking sound and tightened her grip as he broke into a trot.

They followed the bridleway that led from the back of the house and then picked their way up the hill that led to the moor. Suddenly Romeo threw up his head and danced on the spot, impatient to be given his head.

Joanna grinned and touched his mane in a soothing gesture. 'Off you go, then.'

She released the pressure on his head collar and Romeo took off, cantering at first and then extending his pace to a full gallop, the steady thud of his hooves throwing up clods of earth as he moved.

Joanna gave a whoop of delight as they jumped two ditches and increased the pace. Freedom. No one to see her. They galloped for a while and then gradually she slowed the horse, controlling his speed and bringing him to a halt. He was breathing rapidly and she could feel the heat from his flanks burning through the thin fabric of her jodhpurs.

She walked him gently back to the edge of the moor and then back down onto the bridle path, stopping by the river and sliding off his back.

'How about a drink, old chap?' she suggested, removing her hat and rubbing her scalp to loosen her damp hair. It was still early but already she felt hot and sticky. The day was going to be a scorcher.

She stood quietly next to the horse as he stepped gingerly into the water and bent his head to drink.

'Joanna?'

She gave a start and turned, her blue eyes wide. She hadn't known anyone else came here at this time. They didn't usually.

It was Seb, dressed casually in jeans that fitted him like a glove and a black T-shirt that showed off the width and power of his shoulders. He was spectacularly good-looking and her breath caught in her throat.

With a flash of panic she tried to analyse the strength of her reaction to him. She didn't normally notice whether men were good-looking so why was she noticing Seb? And what was he doing here anyway? He was the last person she'd expected to meet. Surely he should have been in bed. *If not his own, then someone else's...*

She swept a hand through her tangled mane of hair, annoyed that he'd disturbed her privacy.

'Did you want something?'

He didn't answer, his attention apparently totally captured by something. She glanced over her shoulder but there was only Romeo, enjoying his paddle in the river. Surely the man had seen a horse before?

Seb started to move towards her, but he obviously wasn't concentrating because he stumbled slightly as his foot hit a rock, almost losing his footing.

Romeo snorted anxiously and Joanna stared at Seb in amazement. What on earth was the matter with him? Why wasn't he looking where he was going? She lifted a hand and soothed the horse gently until he bent his head back down to the water.

Maybe Seb had had too much to drink with Gabby and wasn't entirely sober.

'How was your dinner, Seb?'

He stopped a few feet away from her, still staring. 'Dinner?'

The man was on another planet. 'With Gabby,' she prompted gently, and he blinked.

'Oh, that. Yes, fine.'

Joanna's lips tightened. Poor Gabby probably wouldn't have been pleased to know that she was so forgettable.

Romeo jerked his head and she steadied herself carefully on the slippery rocks, aware that Seb was still staring. And then the penny dropped. He was staring at her.

At her…

'I didn't know you rode.' His voice was slightly hoarse and his eyes seemed to be fixed firmly on her hair. 'I didn't recognise you from a distance.'

She blushed slightly, suddenly realising why he was staring. Because of the way she looked. She raised a hand to her tangled blonde hair again aware that she must look a total mess. Her hair was pretty unmanageable at the best of times, but it was obviously really bad this morning—he couldn't stop looking at it! Well, she certainly wasn't going to apologise. Her early morning rides were for her alone—she didn't intend to start dressing up just in case she met someone on the bridleway.

'I ride when I have the time,' she told him, sliding a hand over Romeo's smooth, warm body, loving the way he felt. 'It's one of the things I do for relaxation.'

'Right.'

Seb seemed unusually short of words and she frowned and gave him an odd look. Normally they were sparring within seconds of meeting, but not this morning. This morning he seemed dumbstruck.

'Seb, if this truce of ours is going to render you speechless, perhaps we'd better think again,' she said gently, and he seemed to shake himself.

'Sorry.' He gave her an apologetic smile and Joanna relaxed slightly and steadied herself against the horse just as Romeo jerked his head, seriously threatening the security of her footing for a second time.

'Well, in any case, it's time I was getting back. I need to shower before surgery.'

She couldn't go anywhere unless he moved, but he was still staring, his cool blue eyes sliding down her body with embarrassing thoroughness.

Suddenly she remembered that she was wearing her revealing bedtime T-shirt tucked into her jodhpurs. She must look utterly ridiculous, with Mickey Mouse grinning inanely on her chest. Not exactly what a man like Seb was used to when looking at a woman!

Well, tough!

She lifted her chin and pulled at Romeo's leading rein, backing him carefully out of the stream before gathering a lump of mane in her hand and vaulting easily onto his back.

Seb walked slowly towards her, a muscle working in his lean jaw as he looked at her through narrowed eyes.

He seemed totally thrown by something but she still couldn't understand what. Surely her messy appearance wasn't enough to affect him so badly?

Maybe he just wasn't a morning person…

'You ought to be getting back, Seb,' she suggested, 'or you'll be late and we've got a busy surgery this morning.'

'Yes.' Still monosyllabic, Seb lifted a hand to pat the horse. 'Do you always ride before surgery?'

'When I can.'

'You're full of surprises, Joanna Weston.' His long, strong fingers rested gently on the horse's neck. 'Why didn't you tell me you rode?'

She shrugged. 'Why should I?'

'No reason.' He grinned. 'But I'm glad to see that you do know how to relax.'

'I do indeed.' Joanna gave a slight smile and ran slim fingers through Romeo's mane. 'Romeo's my relaxation.'

'*Romeo?*' He lifted a dark eyebrow and a muscle flickered in the corner of his mouth. 'Are you serious? Your horse is called Romeo?'

'What's wrong with that?'

He started to laugh. 'Nothing. Nothing at all. Romeo…' He muttered the name under his breath as though he couldn't quite believe it. 'I suppose I should be encouraged that you're capable of showing interest in anything that isn't a pile of books.'

She stiffened defensively and shot him a warning glance. 'We had a truce. Remember?'

'Sorry.' He gave her a sheepish look and then looked at her thoughtfully. 'Do me a favour, though, will you?'

'Very unlikely.' She regarded him curiously. 'But you can try me. What?'

Seb's expression was suddenly serious as he stared up at her. 'Wear your hair down more often. It suits you.'

Her smile faded. Suddenly she felt uncomfortably aware of the way she looked. *And the way he was looking at her.*

'It doesn't fit with my ice maiden image,' she pointed out, and he shook his head slowly.

'It certainly doesn't.' His voice was gruff and his eyes held hers. 'But then we both know that the ice maiden act is just a front.'

Joanna's breathing was suddenly unsteady and she felt incredibly hot. It was the sun, of course—and the fact that she'd been exercising…

She cleared her throat. 'Well, as we're asking for favours here, you can do one for me, too.'

'What's that?'

Her heart was beating fast and her hands suddenly felt clammy. 'You can promise me that you'll shave when you get back to the house.'

'Shave?' Clearly taken aback by her unexpected request, he lifted a hand and stroked long fingers over his hard jaw.

'You look like a pirate, Seb,' she said gruffly, her eyes lingering on the dark stubble on his jaw and then drifting over his broad shoulders and his long, muscular legs. 'My staff will have trouble concentrating if you go to work this morning looking like that.'

There was a long silence and their eyes met.

'And what about you, Joanna?' His voice was soft. 'Will you have trouble concentrating?'

She pulled herself together and managed a cool smile. 'Don't flatter yourself. I'm not interested in men, remember? Only books.'

Normally it was true. She wasn't interested in men. But something about Sebastian Macaulay disturbed her.

It was years since she'd noticed the way a man looked. The first year of medical school, to be precise, but Seb was hard to ignore. Everything about his powerful physique, his blatant masculinity and his careless self-assurance drew attention.

Even hers...

To distance herself from that uncomfortable thought, she urged Romeo into a trot and made her way back towards the paddock, aware that Seb was staring after her.

CHAPTER FOUR

DESPITE Joanna's misgivings, the truce seemed to work.

Sebastian proved himself to be an excellent doctor and surprisingly hard-working, prepared to take on more than his fair share of the workload.

Two weeks later, feeling better than she had for ages, Joanna had to admit that she was glad she hadn't succeeded in chasing him away.

They still had different lifestyles, of course. He was always out during the evening, returning late at night and frequently looking drawn and tired the next morning. But if Joanna thought that he was paying too much attention to his private life, she didn't say anything. They'd agreed on a truce and she was keeping to her side of the bargain. Providing it didn't affect his work.

'What chance do us normal mortals have?' Laura grumbled one morning, tossing a popular newspaper down on Joanna's desk with a sigh. 'Look at her. All legs and boobs.'

Joanna frowned down at the gossip page of the newspaper, focusing in on a picture of Seb with a stunning blonde on his arm. Her eyes flickered to the caption. 'Heir to the Macaulay millions plays the field.'

Well, she could vouch for that. The man seemed to take calls from different women every day of the week. Not that she minded that. The last thing she wanted was to be bumping in to Seb every evening. It would have been hideously awkward.

The small amount of copy under the photo went on to speculate as to whether Seb, now apparently number two in the list of the UK's most eligible bachelors, would ever settle down and marry.

Laura gave a long sigh. 'Doesn't he look fantastic in a dinner jacket? Look at those shoulders…'

Joanna stared at the picture, noting the arrogant tilt of his head and the faint smile on his face as he listened to something his companion was saying. It was a good photograph of him and Laura was right—he did look good in a dinner jacket.

Reading the rest of the article revealed that he had attended a charity ball for disabled children in London. She'd been aware that he hadn't come home the night before, and this explained it.

'Lucky woman,' Laura said gloomily, still staring at the picture. 'What wouldn't I give for one night with a man like him? I bet he's fantastic in bed.'

'Laura!!' Joanna gave her a shocked look and Laura blushed.

'Sorry, Dr Weston, I wasn't thinking. It's just that he's got a way with women and I just—'

'It's all right, Laura.' Joanna interrupted the girl before she could say any more. 'You don't have to explain. Just keep your thoughts to yourself in future, please.'

'Yes, Dr Weston.'

Laura straightened and closed the paper just as Seb tapped on the door and entered the room.

'Joanna, you wanted—' He broke off, his eyes narrowing as he saw the newspaper.

'There's a lovely picture of you in the paper, Dr Macaulay,' Laura said innocently. 'Did you have a nice evening?'

For a moment his mouth tightened and Joanna held her breath, sensing that he was less than pleased to see himself in the paper. But then, to her relief, he smiled, his eyes surprisingly gentle as he looked at the young receptionist.

'I had a very nice evening, thank you, Laura.'

Laura beamed at him and Joanna started to breathe again. 'Did you meet lots of famous people?'

Seb's lips twitched. 'Quite a few,' he murmured. 'Quite a few. Laura, will you excuse us for a moment, please?'

'Oh, of course.' Laura hurried towards the door and left them in peace.

'So…' Joanna sat back in her chair and watched him. 'What happened to Gabby last night, then?'

He frowned slightly. 'Last night was nothing to do with Gabby.'

'Poor Gabby,' Joanna murmured, wondering if the girl knew that her handsome prince had a different girl on his arm every night. *Probably. Especially if she bought newspapers.*

His gaze was slightly questioning. 'It was a fundraising event, Joanna. I get invited to them all the time. It was nothing to do with Gabby.'

Joanna gave a wry smile. 'And it's compulsory to attend with a stunning blonde with legs like a racehorse, of course. What a tough life you lead.'

He strolled across the room towards her, humour lighting his blue eyes. 'The stunning blonde you refer to was actually an old family friend, but I'm intrigued and touched that you're suddenly showing so much interest in my private life, Joanna. You obviously missed me last night.'

Joanna's face heated under his teasing gaze. 'Missed you? Hardly. I didn't even realise you hadn't come home until Laura showed me your picture in the paper this morning.'

It was a lie, of course. She'd been fully aware that he hadn't come home. Over the past two weeks she'd slept really well, reassured by his powerful presence in the house. Last night, all on her own for the first time for a while, she'd hardly got any sleep at all.

Seb threw his head back and laughed. 'Joanna, I'm crushed. And there was I telling myself that our relationship had progressed to a new footing and that you were suddenly seeing me in a whole new light.'

'Let's not delude ourselves,' Joanna said dryly. 'I admit that our truce seems to have worked and that we seem to have managed to develop a tolerable working relationship, but let's not get carried away here. You and I are complete opposites and we always will be.'

Seb shrugged, a strange light in his eyes. 'They say that opposites attract…'

Attract?

Suddenly she remembered Laura's comment about him being good in bed. She closed her eyes briefly and took a deep breath. *What was happening to her?*

'Are you all right?' He was looking at her with an odd expression in his eyes, and she quickly pulled herself together.

'Fine. Just a bit tired. Look, I wanted to—'

'Why are you tired?' He picked up on her remark immediately, his gaze searching. 'Didn't you sleep last night?'

'Not as well as usual,' she admitted, and his gaze sharpened.

'Because I was away?' Understanding dawned and he cursed under his breath. 'Damn. I hadn't thought of that.'

She should have denied her fear, told him that he'd misunderstood—but something in those blue eyes was so concerned and kind that she couldn't bring herself to lie.

'Crazy, isn't it?' she mumbled, embarrassed by her own weakness, but he shook his head, his expression grim.

'No, it isn't crazy, Joanna. But maybe I'll take a look at the security arrangements while I'm here, and have a word with George.'

'I spoke to him last night.' Joanna's face brightened and

she seized on the opportunity to change the subject. 'He says the baby is doing quite well.'

'That's good.' Seb gave a nod and then checked his watch. 'Anyway, you wanted to talk to me about something—you left me a note?'

She had left him a note. And she'd totally forgotten about it from the moment he'd strolled into her consulting room. *She was losing her mind.*

'It's a work issue.'

His lips twitched. 'Of course.'

'Seb!' She lifted an eyebrow warningly. 'I haven't said anything about you partying until dawn…'

'OK, OK.' He lifted his hands in a gesture of surrender and settled himself comfortably in the chair next to her desk. 'Go on, then. Fire away.'

For someone who *had* been partying until dawn he looked disgustingly fresh and handsome. Joanna pushed the thought away quickly. She did *not* find Seb Macaulay handsome.

'You've got a Mr Peters on your list this morning.'

'Have I?'

'Yes.' She licked dry lips. 'And I've asked Laura to send him through to see me instead.'

Seb frowned, the humour fading from his eyes. 'Is he your patient?'

'No, but—'

'And has he asked to see you?'

'No, but—'

'Then he stays on my list,' Seb said, his voice suddenly cool. 'How do you know he didn't ask for a male doctor intentionally? It's not just women that like to consult members of their own sex, you know.'

Joanna silently counted to ten. 'Dr Macaulay, I've been working in this practice for three years and I think I know these patients a little better than you. There are issues in that family that you don't know about.'

'So…' He shrugged with that careless arrogance that she found so infuriating. 'Brief me on them, then.'

Joanna opened her mouth to argue with him and then closed it again. Her first patient was due in less than five minutes. She didn't have time for confrontation.

'All right. If you insist on being obstructive. His wife, Vera, is my patient,' she told him, worry creasing her brow as she thought about the old lady. 'She's normally an affable enough person, no real problems. She came to see me a week ago with something minor and she was making all sorts of accusations about her husband.'

Seb was listening carefully. 'What sort of accusations?'

Joanna shrugged. 'She said he was stealing her things, hiding things from her…'

'How old are they?'

'They're both in their early eighties.'

'And neither of them have had any obvious health problems that could have led to confusion?'

'No. Not that I'm aware of.'

'So I need to mention this to him and see what he says,' Seb murmured, his expression thoughtful. 'All right. I'll let you know what I think.'

It was lunchtime by the time she finished her morning list and walked through to Reception to pick up her house calls from Laura.

'Has Dr Macaulay finished yet?'

She was anxious to hear how he'd got on with Mr Peters.

'He's on his last patient,' Laura told her, 'and he's been in there for ages.'

Joanna glanced at her watch. At least he was thorough.

'Only two calls, Laura?' She scanned the list, surprised that it was so short.

'Don't complain.' Seb strolled into the reception area and smiled at Laura. 'Sorry to overrun.'

Laura turned pink. 'Doesn't matter, Dr Macaulay. You were on your last patient anyway. I've just had a call from Mrs Hunt up at Moorland Cottages. She's really worried about little Elliot. He's had a raging temperature since last night and he's really listless. She wondered if you'd call.'

Seb nodded. 'How old is he?'

'Three,' Joanna said quickly, reaching for the notes. 'I'll do it. I delivered Elliot at home in my first week in the job and I know the family really well.'

'You know every family really well,' Seb said quietly, picking up his bag. 'And I'm quite capable of doing the visit.'

'I know that.' Joanna flushed and bit her lip. She really wasn't trying to offend him but the patients were like her family and she couldn't bear not to be involved in their care. They needed her. *And she needed them...*

Seb gave a sigh. 'Look, I know you had problems with your last locum but you should know by now that I'm not him. As there are only three calls, why don't we do them together? That way you get to see Elliot and I get to meet a few more of your patients.'

Joanna looked at him doubtfully. 'Isn't that a waste of manpower?'

'Probably,' he agreed gently, 'but as you don't seem able to delegate, and I refuse to allow you to take over my workload as well as your own, we don't seem to have much choice. We can talk about patients on the way and call it a practice meeting if it makes you feel better.'

Without giving her time to answer, he gave Laura a quick smile and strode out of the surgery.

Joanna stared after him, knowing that his accusation was fair. She *did* have trouble delegating. Giving herself a quick shake, she followed him, jogging to catch up with him as he walked across the car park.

He paused beside his car, not commenting on the fact that she'd decided to join him. 'Is she a panicky mother or is it likely to be serious?'

'She's the most laid-back mother in the practice,' Joanna told him as he scanned her worried expression.

'In that case, let's take my car. It's faster.'

For once she didn't waste time disagreeing with him, and within seconds they were speeding along the road towards the house where the Hunt family lived.

Mr Hunt was hovering by the doorway, his face strained. He breathed a visible sigh of relief as the car pulled up.

'Dr Weston, thank goodness you've come. It's Elliot—'

Joanna hurried past him into the house, aware that Seb was close behind her. 'Where is he?'

'Upstairs in his room. Second on the right.'

They hurried up the stairs two at a time and pushed open the door of the bedroom.

'He's getting sicker by the minute.' Mrs Hunt was as pale as her husband, her face anguished as she looked at the toddler who was lying still and pale on the bed. 'He's not even crying any more.'

While Seb quickly examined the child, Joanna took a history from the mother.

'When did it start, Sue?'

'Just last night,' she whispered, biting her lip. 'He was fine during the day and then late last night he suddenly started being sick and his temperature went up. I just thought he'd picked something up—you know what they're like at this age. But then he started to say that his head hurt.'

Seb finished his examination and reached into his bag. 'He's a very sick little boy, Mrs Hunt,' he said quietly. 'I think there's a strong possibility that he has meningitis. I

want to give him an injection of penicillin immediately and
then he needs to be admitted to hospital so that they can
run some tests.'

'Meningitis?' Sue turned to look at Joanna, her eyes wide
with horror. 'It can't be! He was fine yesterday.'

Joanna glanced at Seb but it was clear from his grim
expression that he was in little doubt about his diagnosis.

'It can happen very quickly,' Joanna said gently, removing her mobile phone from her pocket, knowing that speed
was essential. Elliot needed to be in hospital. 'Dr Macaulay
will give him some penicillin while I call an ambulance
and talk to the hospital.'

She stepped outside the room briefly to make the call,
speaking first to Ambulance Control and then to the hospital. When she walked back into the room Seb was talking
to Sue.

'Is he allergic to penicillin?' Seb drew up the injection
as he asked the question.

Sue shook her head, raising a shaking hand to her mouth.
'No. No he isn't. But how do we know it's that? He hasn't
got a rash. The leaflets talk about rashes—'

'Not everyone gets a rash,' Seb told her, checking the
dose of penicillin and injecting it quickly. 'And we don't
know for sure that it's meningitis, but we give penicillin
anyway, just in case. If it turns out to be something else,
the penicillin won't have done any harm.'

'But how can it be meningitis? He's been vaccinated.'

'There are several different organisms that cause meningitis,' Seb explained carefully. 'If he had all his immu-
nisations as a baby then he's probably protected against
meningitis group C and haemophilus influenza, but there
are other types.'

'I've spoken to the doctor on the paediatric ward and
they're expecting him,' Joanna told them, slipping the
phone back into her bag. 'And the ambulance is on its way.'

She watched as Seb moved closer to Sue, his eyes fixed on her tense profile.

'You've done all the right things, Mrs Hunt,' he said softly, lifting a hand and placing it on her shoulder.

She shook her head, choking back the tears. 'I should have called you last night.'

'No.' Seb's voice was firm and reassuring. 'You had no reason to call us last night. This disease can strike frighteningly quickly and you did really well to call us when you did.'

Sue turned to face him, her expression tormented. 'But if I *had* called you last night…'

Seb shrugged. 'I probably wouldn't have thought it was serious either,' he said quietly. 'You're a good and caring mother and you've done everything you possibly can. Now you just need to concentrate on giving him the support he needs. Will you go with him in the ambulance?'

Sue nodded. 'Yes. If they'll let me.'

Joanna looked at Seb with new respect. It hadn't even occurred to her that Sue could possibly be blaming herself. *But it had occurred to Seb.* And he'd done his best to stop the young mother feeling guilty.

The shriek of the ambulance siren disturbed her thoughts.

'They're here.' Sue glanced at her husband, suddenly flustered. 'I need to pack a bag—'

'I'll come back and pack you one later, love.' Her husband gave her a brief hug and then scooped up his sleeping son from the bed. 'Let's get the lad to hospital now as fast as we can.'

'If it is meningitis, we'll need to trace his contacts and give them antibiotics,' Seb said as they walked downstairs. 'The hospital will talk to you about it.'

'We've hardly seen anyone lately,' Sue said, scraping her hair out of her eyes, dazed with worry. 'Elliot is due to start nursery in September but at the moment he's just at home with me.'

'Well, the hospital may need to give you something,' Seb told her, opening the front door and walking up to the paramedics.

While Seb briefed them, Joanna helped Sue settle herself in the ambulance.

As the vehicle pulled away, roaring down the country road as fast as they safely could, Joanna let out a deep breath and walked back towards the car, feeling totally drained. If anything happened to little Elliot…

She turned to Seb, needing his reassurance even though she knew that he couldn't give it. 'Do you think he'll be all right?'

His eyes were surprisingly gentle. 'I don't know, Joanna. Your knowledge of medicine is as good as mine. We both know that bacterial meningitis has a mortality rate of more than ten per cent. But we've given him penicillin,' he reminded her, 'and we've got him to hospital as early as we could. There's nothing more anyone could have done. Now we just have to hope.'

Joanna sank into the soft leather of the passenger seat, her mind still on little Elliot.

'If anything happens to him…' suddenly she felt a lump building in her throat and she clenched her teeth and fought for control. The last thing she wanted to do was cry in front of Seb. She couldn't think of anything more embarrassing.

'Let's be optimistic,' Seb murmured, reversing the car out of the drive and then roaring back along the road. 'And let's hope the next two calls aren't so stressful.'

They weren't, and in less than twenty minutes they were climbing back in the car again and heading for the surgery.

Or at least that was where they were supposed to be heading…

Joanna frowned as she watched the countryside flash by. 'The surgery isn't this way. You've taken a wrong turning.'

'I'm not going to the surgery.'

'What do you mean?' She looked at him but he was concentrating on the narrow roads, his strong hands holding the wheel steady as he negotiated the corners. 'Where are we going, then?'

'We're going for lunch, Joanna.'

'Lunch?' He swung the car into the car park of a country pub that she didn't even recognise. They certainly weren't anywhere near the surgery. 'But I don't want lunch. I don't take a lunch break.'

He switched off the engine and turned to look at her, his expression mildly amused. 'Well, I do, and you're in my car.'

She gaped at him. 'But I've got work to do.'

'Work...' he closed his eyes briefly. 'Your favourite word. Let's leave work behind for half an hour, Jo. We've got phones. They can call us if there's a crisis.'

'But—'

He lifted a finger and touched her lips gently. '*But* is your second-favourite word, did you know that?' He paused, his finger still resting on the softness of her mouth, and she swallowed hard and moved away, his touch making her feel odd.

'I'm not really hungry. I'm too worried about Elliot to eat anything—'

'Well, fainting from hunger isn't going to help the little chap,' Seb pointed out, opening his door and climbing out of the car.

Joanna hesitated and then her door was opened and he was looking down at her quizzically.

'Are you coming in or are you going to wait for me in the car?'

Wait for him in the car? How could she do that?

She climbed out and glared at him. 'You really haven't given me any choice, have you?'

'No.' He smiled placidly and she shifted uncomfortably under that steady gaze.

'Well, if we're really stopping for lunch it has to be a quickie.'

His eyes gleamed wickedly. 'If that's your preference. I prefer something a little more leisurely myself.'

She blushed hotly and gritted her teeth, trying not to let him see how much his laughing comment had unsettled her. 'You are so infuriating—'

'Oh, come on, Joanna.' His voice was a low drawl and he flicked her cheek with a finger. 'Loosen up a bit, will you? You can do it if you try.'

She ignored him and stalked across to the entrance of the pub, her attention suddenly arrested by the colourful plants cascading out of terracotta pots on a scrubbed stone patio.

'Oh…' She stopped dead, breathing in the heady scent of the flowers and feeling the warmth of the summer sun touching her skin.

'Nice, isn't it?'

She bit her lip and turned to look at Seb, knowing that she should be angry with the way he'd outmanoeuvred her, but as her eyes met his she suddenly forgot everything she'd intended to say.

Suddenly all she was aware of was the thickness of his lashes and the dark masculinity of his jawline.

Their eyes held and then his gaze flickered to her mouth. For a wild moment, she thought he might kiss her, but then he straightened and waved a hand at the tables.

'Shall we sit outside?'

'Good idea.' Her voice cracked slightly and she cleared her throat, shaken by the unfamiliar feelings that were taking over her body. She was going mad. Had she really thought he'd kiss her? Ridiculous! Men like Seb Macaulay didn't kiss women like her.

He shrugged off his jacket and slung it carelessly over the seat. 'You sit down and I'll fetch us a menu and something to drink.'

Joanna settled herself at the table and glanced round guiltily. She never, ever stopped working at lunchtime. Never. It was a totally alien experience. What if someone saw her? Having lunch when she should be working...

So what if someone saw them? She was allowed to stop for lunch. It was just that usually she didn't have time. Or the inclination.

Seb returned with drinks and settled himself at the table. 'I decided to risk your wrath and order for us before it gets busy in there. Brie and bacon baguettes all right with you?'

'Fine, thanks.' If Seb was expecting her to argue with him, he was going to be disappointed. She was fast learning that it wasn't worth arguing with him.

He took a large mouthful of his drink. 'Do you seriously never stop for lunch? Even when George was here?'

'No.' She gave him a warning look. 'And before you say anything derogatory, remember our truce. You're not allowed to mention my working habits, remember?'

'I remember!' He smiled and held up his hands in a gesture of surrender. 'I remember. It's funny really, isn't it, you and I being thrown together like this?'

'Riotous,' Joanna said lightly, taking a sip of her drink and smiling as the waitress brought their food. 'Thank you very much.'

'So come on, then...' Seb tore a piece off his baguette and chewed thoughtfully. 'Tell me something about yourself that I don't already know.'

She frowned at him. 'What do you mean? You know it all already. I trained in London, like you, I worked in—'

'I said tell me something I don't know,' he interrupted

her impatiently. 'I don't want to talk about work. I want to talk about you. Tell me something *personal* about yourself. Apart from the fact that you like animals.'

She blushed hotly. Personal? 'I don't like talking about my personal life.'

Especially not with Seb Macaulay. She could just imagine what he'd have to say about the state of her personal life.

'Why?' His gaze was uncomfortably direct. 'Why, Joanna? Why don't you like talking about yourself?'

'I just don't,' she muttered, and he leaned across the table towards her, his voice suddenly soft.

'You intrigue me, do you know that? I used to think that maybe you just weren't capable of deep emotion, but I know that's not true because I've seen the way you are with your patients.'

'Seb, please…'

'No, let me finish, Joanna.' His eyes were locked firmly with hers. 'In the last week I've seen a completely different side to you, and what I want to know is why it's only your patients that see those qualities. What are you hiding from? Or should I say, *who* are you hiding from?'

She glanced at him, startled, thinking once more that he was unusually perceptive. 'No one. I'm not hiding…'

'Yes, you are.' His gaze held hers for a long moment and then he sat back in his chair, still watching her thoughtfully. 'Was it a man?'

Hot colour flooded her cheeks again. 'That is none of your business.'

'No, you're right, it isn't,' he agreed, taking a slug of his drink. 'It isn't my business, except that I hate to see you burying yourself in your work as a form of protection. I just wonder what you're protecting yourself from.'

Joanna felt tears prick her eyes and cursed herself. What on earth was the matter? She wasn't usually this sensitive.

'If you've finished your lunch, I'd like to get back to work, Dr Macaulay.' Joanna stood up quickly and Seb immediately reached out a hand and caught her wrist.

'Joanna, I'm sorry.' Strong fingers tightened on her flesh. 'I was out of line and I apologise. I wasn't being nosy. Just concerned.'

Concerned? Why would he be concerned about her?

She stared at him blankly. 'I don't need your concern, Seb.'

His smile was wry. 'Well you've got it anyway, but never mind that now. Sit down again. Please. You haven't finished your sandwich.'

She hesitated and then did as he requested. What choice did she have? She'd come in his car.

'I tell you what.' Seb's tone was light. 'To make amends for prying, you can ask me any question of your choice, no matter how personal.'

Joanna smothered a smile, wondering what the gossip columnists would make of an offer like that.

'Actually, there is something I've always wondered about you,' she confessed, and he looked at her in mock horror.

'Be gentle with me.'

She looked at him seriously. 'Why did someone like you become a doctor?'

One dark eyebrow lifted. 'Someone like me? Someone wealthy, you mean? It isn't mandatory to fritter away your life just because you're fortunate enough to have family money, you know.'

Joanna took a sip of her drink. 'But why didn't you join your family's business?'

He shrugged. 'Because I wanted to do medicine. Ever since I was small I wanted to study medicine.'

'And your family didn't mind?'

'Oh, they minded.' Seb gave a short laugh and fiddled

with his glass. 'They minded a lot. In fact, they tried their hardest to put me off, but when they didn't succeed they were eventually forced to accept that they had a potential doctor in the family, not an heir apparent to the Macaulay business.'

'So who runs the business now?'

'My younger brother and my sister, along with my father.'

'And you won't ever change your mind?'

Seb shook his head. 'No way. I love medicine too much.'

'But you're not building a career as such, you just flit from job to job,' she began, and then broke off, embarrassed. 'I'm sorry. That sounded terribly rude. And I broke our truce.'

He laughed. 'Well, seeing that I've already done that once this lunchtime, it makes us quits. And the answer to your question is that the practice of medicine isn't necessarily restricted to building a high-profile career for oneself. I like the variety of what I do and it suits me not to be tied down.'

Of course it did.

Why should his answer disappoint her so much? She'd always known what sort of man he was and no one could deny that he was pulling his weight in the practice, so why should she care that he'd be moving on in a few months' time?

'So where were you before the cruise?'

He hesitated. 'I was in South America,' he said finally, avoiding her gaze as he stood up and delved into his pocket for his wallet. 'Come on, we ought to be going.'

Joanna sensed that the subject was closed but she was suddenly curious. Why was he so reluctant to talk about his past work? Because he was afraid she'd dismiss it as trivial?

She reached into her bag for some money and handed him a note. 'I want to pay for mine.'

He frowned, not taking the note. 'I don't think—'

'This was two colleagues having lunch, Seb,' she reminded him crisply, 'not a date. I want to pay for myself.'

'Fine.' He reached out and took the money without further argument, and minutes later they were back in the car.

Seb settled himself in the driver's seat, pressed a button and the roof slid smoothly away.

'What are you doing?' Joanna's voice was filled with disapproval. 'We're not on holiday, Seb. Have you forgotten we're supposed to be working?'

'Am I likely to forget, with you as a partner?' His tone was dry as he started the engine. 'I'm trying to show you that it's possible to mix work and pleasure. Come on, Joanna, live a little. It's a bright, sunny day. You're about to experience life in a sports car with the roof down. Relax. You might even enjoy it.'

She did enjoy it.

More than she would ever have imagined or dared to admit.

With a sigh of pleasure she leaned her head back against the soft leather and closed her eyes.

'It's a great car, isn't it?'

It *was* a great car. And being driven in it was a totally hedonistic experience. The richness of the soft leather, the warmth of the sun on her face, the wind in her hair—all combined to make her feel strangely euphoric.

All too soon Seb pulled up outside the surgery and Joanna lifted a hand to her hair self-consciously, suddenly aware that her brief interlude of pleasure was over.

'Goodness, I must look a real mess…'

His mouth twitched. 'Joanna, nothing could make a mess of your hair when it's pinned up like that. It couldn't escape if it tried. I had no idea what your hair looked like until I saw you riding the other day.'

For a brief moment his gaze locked on hers and he reached out to touch her hair. 'And the truth is, you have beautiful hair. Gorgeous hair. Hair that should be loose and free. Why do you always scrape it back?'

Beautiful hair? He thought she had *beautiful hair?*

'I prefer it scraped back,' she muttered, wishing that he'd move his hand. She was starting to feel strange and she couldn't work out why. 'It looks more professional like this.'

'It's all part of your armour, isn't it?' he murmured softly, fingering a stray curl thoughtfully. 'Just like your job.'

'I don't know what you mean, and we're going to be late for surgery.' She shifted back in her seat so that he was forced to remove his hand.

'Surgery.' He looked at her steadily, a ghost of a smile playing around his firm mouth. 'When did you last have fun, Jo? When did you last let your hair down, apart from with your horse?'

Joanna fumbled for the doorhandle, determined to get away from him as quickly as possible. He seemed to be carefully unravelling every detail of her life as if it were a wool jumper and he'd found a loose thread. If she wasn't careful her protection would fall away completely and her feelings would be left totally exposed.

Without answering him, she stumbled out of the car and crunched her way across the gravel of the car park, barely pausing to greet Laura as she hurried into her consulting room.

Immediately the door opened again and Seb strode in, closing it firmly behind him.

'Joanna, listen—'

'You were the one who called a truce.' She glared at him

accusingly from behind the safety of her desk. 'You! You said that you wouldn't comment on my lifestyle if I didn't comment on yours.'

A muscle worked in his jaw. 'I know that, but—'

'But what?' She raised her small chin defiantly. 'What gives you the right to change your own rules? Because you think you know how to improve my life? Well, let me tell you something, *Dr Macaulay*, I'm very happy with my life. Every part of it. And that *includes the way I wear my hair*.'

'OK, OK.' He lifted his hands in a gesture of surrender. 'I apologise unreservedly and I promise not to make any more comments about your hair.'

'Good. Well, in that case, if you'll excuse me, I've got patients to see.'

'Patients.' He gave a wry smile and ran long fingers across his smooth forehead. 'OK, Joanna, you win. The conversation is safely back to the topic of work. In which case, we may as well start with John Peters.'

Joanna hesitated, finding it hard to think about work let alone discuss it. Her mind was in a total jumble. 'What about him?'

'I saw him this morning.'

Of course he had. She'd totally forgotten. She shook her head slightly in the hope that the fog might clear. 'So— what did you think?'

'Well, it's a tricky situation, there's no doubt about that.' Seb strolled across to her window and stared out across the car park to the moor beyond. 'He claimed that Vera is imagining it all.'

Joanna sighed. 'I was afraid that would be the case. So now what?'

'I suppose we have to consider whether one or both of them might be suffering from some form of dementia. The incidence of dementia in the over-80 age group is about 20 per cent, isn't it? Are there any other family members who could shed some light?'

'A son,' Joanna told him quickly, 'but he doesn't live in the village. What did John say about her accusations of stealing?'

'He denied it all.'

'OK.' Joanna gave a resigned shrug. 'In that case, we'll just have to keep an eye on them. I'll find an excuse to call. The poor things. It's no fun getting old, is it?'

Seb's eyes clashed with hers. 'All the more reason to have fun when you're young,' he said softly, and she swallowed hard.

'I thought we'd agreed to drop that subject. I've already told you that I like my life, Seb,' she muttered, and he gave a short laugh.

'I suspect that that's because you don't know what you're missing.'

She shot him an irritated look and stood up, walking briskly to the door, hoping that he'd take the hint and leave. He was getting much too interested in her private life for her liking. 'I'm not missing anything, Seb,' she said tartly, 'except the opportunity to get on with my work because I'm chatting with you.'

His voice was filled with pure, undiluted exasperation. 'Joanna, do you *ever* think about anything other than work?'

Joanna started to speak, but without warning he jerked her towards him and his mouth collided with hers so swiftly that she was taken totally by surprise. For a brief second she stood, frozen with shock, aware only of the hardness of his body against hers and the teasing, coaxing pressure of his lips. In a fog of unfamiliar sensations she felt him lift his hands and cup her face, angling it gently but firmly so that he had better access. Only when his tongue gently traced the seam of her mouth did she come to her senses and try and voice her outrage at his actions. It was the wrong thing to do. As her mouth opened he deepened the kiss and her knees immediately gave way, as weak and useless as if she'd drunk an entire bottle of champagne in one mouthful.

He kissed her so slowly and so thoroughly that by the time he eventually released her she was so dazed that she could barely focus on him, let alone put him in his place. It was the sort of kiss she'd imagined only ever happened in books and films, never in real life. The sort of kiss that young girls dreamed of. The sort of kiss that would have woken a sleeping princess.

She stumbled away from him, touching her tingling lips with shaking fingers.

'What the hell do you think you're doing?'

There was a long silence and when Joanna finally plucked up the courage to look at Seb his expression was impossible to read.

'Kissing you, Joanna.' His voice sounded strange. 'I was kissing you.'

Her heart was doing a war dance in her chest. 'I know that. I meant, *why?*'

What possible reason was there for him to have kissed her?

'Why?' He paused, his eyes scanning her as if she were a stranger he'd never met before. 'Because I wanted to stop you talking about work.'

She ran the tip of her tongue over her mouth, trying to soothe the strange feelings his lips had triggered. 'You're crazy…'

'Am I?' His eyes dropped to her mouth, resting for a long moment on the fullness of her lips, and she swallowed hard, confused by the feelings that were erupting inside her.

'Well, next time you want to stop me talking about work, just try changing the subject.' Her voice was hoarse and his eyes flickered up to hers, a strange expression lighting their blue depths.

'I think that's what I just did,' he said softly, and then turned on his heel and left the room.

CHAPTER FIVE

HE'D kissed Joanna Weston.

Seb closed the door of his consulting room and closed his eyes briefly, remembering her shocked response when his mouth had taken possession of hers, the sweet taste of her lips as she'd opened them to him.

Damn.

He ran a hand over his face and took a deep breath, trying to pull himself together. He'd lost count of the number of women he'd kissed since he'd reached adolescence, and he'd thought he'd moved beyond the stage of being bowled over by one kiss.

So why did he feel like a hormone-drenched teenager?

And why had he done it? What on earth had possessed him to kiss Joanna? Up until a week ago he hadn't even *liked* her, and he certainly hadn't found her attractive.

But that was because he'd never taken the trouble to get to know the real Joanna before, he admitted. Like all his colleagues in medical school, he'd written her off as bookish and prim, with no interest in her fellow man.

But he'd been wrong.

Very wrong.

You only had to see the way her patients adored her to realise that there were hidden depths to Joanna. Underneath that frosty exterior she was warm and caring and very, very vulnerable.

And intriguing…

He walked across to his desk and sat down, trying to push away the feeling that they'd all been unfair to her. He'd always prided himself on never taking anyone or any-

90

thing at face value. After all, he hated it when people did the same thing to him, and he knew that they did. Plenty of people had been ready to dismiss him as a rich man's son who was just playing at medicine.

He stared at his afternoon list of patients without seeing it. He knew without a shadow of a doubt that Joanna was hiding a large part of herself away, that she was using her work as a form of protection. But the question was, what or who was she protecting herself from?

Cursing softly, he forced his mind back to his work. It was none of his business. She'd made it clear enough that she didn't want him interfering in her private life. And why did he even want to?

He pushed aside memories of her soft body melting into his, of the look in her wide, blue eyes as she'd gazed at him after the kiss. She'd been shocked. Stunned.

With a wry smile he buzzed for his first patient, wondering what she'd say if she knew that he felt exactly the same way.

Joanna stared out of the window. It was as if her entire world had shifted and nothing made sense any more.

One kiss.

One kiss was all it had taken to show her that she wasn't the person she'd thought she was. She searched her brain for some logical explanation for her response to the man. But there wasn't one. What she'd felt—*what he'd made her feel*—wasn't something that could be neatly explained away by logic.

It was as if a kaleidoscope of new colours had suddenly erupted into her life, and she didn't recognise any of them. She'd never thought that she was the sort of woman who was capable of those feelings.

The door suddenly opened and she turned in mute panic, sagging with relief when she saw that it was Laura.

'Are you all right, Dr Weston? You're as white as a sheet.' Laura hurried across to her and Joanna gave her a weak smile as she flicked on her computer.

'I'm fine, Laura,' she lied, and Laura paused, looking at her doubtfully before handing her a piece of paper.

'Mrs King from Plough Lane called and wanted to speak to you about her diarrhoea. Those tablets you prescribed aren't working and she wondered if you could give her anything else.'

Joanna stared at the piece of paper blankly, her mind refusing to function.

Laura looked at her curiously. 'I said you'd call her at the end of surgery.'

'Yes.' Joanna gave a slow nod. 'Yes, of course I will. Thank you, Laura.'

Laura frowned. 'Dr Weston, are you sure you're all right? You don't seem like yourself at all.'

She wasn't herself. In fact, she didn't have the faintest idea who she was any more.

'Are you worrying about little Elliot?' Laura gave a sympathetic sigh. 'I'm crossing my fingers he'll be all right. Dr Macaulay just phoned the hospital and they said that Elliot is in Intensive Care but stable.'

Joanna's head jerked up at that piece of news. Seb had phoned the hospital? The kiss obviously hadn't put him off his work, then.

And why should it?

Why should one little kiss with someone as inexperienced as her put Seb off his work? He kissed women all the time. It was hardly likely to have affected him the same way it had affected her...

'Are you ready for your first patient, Dr Weston?' Laura was hovering by the door and Joanna pulled herself together and nodded.

'Yes.' She leaned forward and pressed the buzzer on her

desk, telling herself that work would soon take her mind off her problems. After all, it had always worked in the past.

Her first patient was an eight-year-old boy who suffered from eczema and whom she saw on a fairly regular basis.

'Hello, Freddie.' She gave him a warm smile and then glanced at his mother, who was hovering anxiously by the door. 'Come on in, Mrs Dover. How are things?'

'Not great, to be honest, Dr Weston.' Mrs Dover pushed Freddie forward. 'Show Dr Weston your skin, pet.'

Freddie scowled and reluctantly removed his T-shirt.

Joanna winced slightly as she examined the angry rash on his body. 'You've been scratching, Freddie,' she said gently, and he stared at her mutinously.

'It itches.'

'I know it does,' she said softly, 'but the more you scratch it the more it will itch.'

She took another look at his skin, noting that the constant scratching had caused some lichenification.

'He's not sleeping, Dr Weston,' his mother told her, 'and when he does fall asleep he's scratching. I'm at my wits' end.'

'How often do you have a bath, Freddie?'

Freddie shifted slightly. 'I hate baths.'

Joanna nodded, hiding the smile. 'Most boys of your age do,' she said lightly, 'but for you it isn't about being clean, it's about stopping the itch. We need to make sure that your skin is well oiled. How much emollient is he using, Mrs Dover?'

Mrs Dover sighed. 'Not as much as he should do, and I suppose that's my fault. I should make him have his baths.'

'He needs emollient in the bath and after the bath,' Joanna reminded them, tapping the computer and waiting while a prescription printed out. 'Take this to the chemist. It's a prescription for an emollient that contains lauromacrogols. It should help the itch. Now then, Freddie…' She turned to the little boy, her face serious. 'Instead of scratching, I want you to learn to pat.'

He looked at her blankly. 'Pat?'

'Uh-huh.' She nodded vigorously. 'Instead of using your nails on your skin, I want you to try patting it. Try it now.'

His expression was doubtful but he did as he was told and she beamed at him.

'Good boy. Now, next time you feel like scratching I want you to stop yourself and pat the skin instead. Show me your nails.'

Freddie held out his hands and Joanna examined them and glanced up at his mother.

'They could be a bit shorter. It might help. When you get home I suggest you cut his nails so that he's less likely to damage his skin if he does scratch. What's he wearing in this warm weather?'

Mrs Dover picked up the discarded T-shirt. 'Cotton mostly, like this. We do try and avoid synthetic fabrics.'

'That's great.' Joanna nodded her approval. 'And no soaps or detergents in the bath?'

Freddie shook his head. 'I don't often have baths.'

Joanna looked at him severely. 'Well, you must. You don't have to use soap, but you do have to have baths. Baths help the itching. Promise me, Freddie?'

Freddie gave her a sheepish grin. 'OK.'

'Good boy.' Joanna glanced up at Mrs Dover. 'What we're really trying to do here is to reduce water loss from the skin by using plenty of emollients, and break the itch-scratch cycle that's developed. The more he scratches, the more he'll itch. If you see him scratching, try and encourage him to pat the skin instead. What we have to do is break the habit of scratching.'

Mrs Dover smiled gratefully and helped Freddie wriggle back into his T-shirt. 'Thanks, Dr Weston.'

'No problem.'

Joanna waited for them to go and then buzzed for her next patient.

Wendy Hill was an anxious-looking woman in her mid-thirties. Joanna had seen her a few times over the years with minor problems.

'Hello, Wendy.' Joanna greeted her warmly. 'What can I do for you today?'

Wendy shifted slightly in her chair and coloured slightly. 'Mick and I have been trying for a baby...'

'I see.' Joanna murmured. 'And so far nothing has happened?'

Wendy's eyes filled. 'Ridiculous, isn't it? I spent the whole of my twenties praying that I wouldn't get pregnant, and now I'm spending the whole of my thirties praying that I will.'

Joanna gave a sympathetic chuckle. 'I know. You're not alone in thinking that, I can assure you. I'm going to need to ask you a few questions and then we can work out what tests—if any—we need to do. OK?'

Wendy nodded. 'I tried to get Mick to come with me but he was too embarrassed. He just wants to leave it to nature.'

'Well, that's my first question,' Joanna said gently. 'Contrary to popular belief, it can take quite a while for a woman to become pregnant. How long have you and Mick been trying?'

'Two years, and I'm thirty-five now,' Wendy said gloomily. 'I'm going to be too old soon. I wish I could put the clock back. I spent all those years on my career thinking that I had plenty of time for babies, and now that I've decided I want them I'm terribly afraid that I've left it too long.'

'Are you working at the moment?'

'Yes. I've got a very pressured sales job and I'm away a lot. But we still manage to make love,' she added hastily, turning red again. 'We do it every month at exactly the right time. I make sure that I'm never away in my fertile period.'

'Well, that in itself can be stressful. Concentrating exclusively on your fertile period can put a strain on your relationship,' Joanna said. 'If you can, it's better just to make love regularly throughout the month—whenever you feel like it.'

Wendy sighed. 'You sound like Mick. He says that all he is at the moment is a baby machine, and not a very effective one at that.'

Joanna gave an understanding nod. 'I know it's easy to say and less easy to do, but you have to try and relax. Now then, I just need to ask you some questions about your own history.'

She checked that Wendy had no medical problems and that she had no history of sexually transmitted disease. Then she questioned her about her periods and gave her a full examination.

'Well, everything seems fine so far, Wendy,' she reassured the young woman as she sat back down at her desk. 'What I want to do now is a series of blood tests taken at different times throughout your menstrual cycle, which will tell me what your hormones are doing.'

Wendy listened while Joanna told her when to come back and have bloods taken.

'And what about Mick?'

'He needs to give us a sperm sample.' Joanna explained the reasons and gathered together the appropriate forms. 'Do you think he'll agree to do that?'

'He won't be given any choice,' Wendy said stoutly, bending down and picking up her handbag. 'If I'm having all these tests, I don't see why he can't, too.'

Joanna smiled. 'Well, let's get the tests done and then

we can have another meeting and discuss the results and where we go from here.'

'Thanks, Dr Weston.'

Joanna moved on to her next patient, and by the time she'd finished her surgery she was feeling much more in control again.

It had just been a kiss, for goodness' sake. It had meant nothing at all. Certainly not to Seb who was probably as careless about where he bestowed his kisses as he was with everything else in his life. And she needn't worry about the way she'd responded. He'd just caught her unawares.

She walked through to Reception and noticed that there were two patients waiting.

'Both for Dr Macaulay,' Laura said, intercepting her glance, and Joanna smiled.

'Thanks, Laura. In that case, I'm off.'

With unusual haste she hurried back through the surgery and into the house, deciding to make herself scarce before Seb finished surgery. She didn't want to see him yet. It was too embarrassing. She needed time to get her thoughts straight.

She dragged on her jodhpurs, thrust her riding hat on her head and sprinted down the stairs in a matter of minutes, determined to leave the house before he entered it. Knowing Seb, he'd have plans for the evening so as long as she stayed out of the house for a couple of hours there should be no chance of bumping into him.

He was waiting for her when she got back from her ride, one foot resting casually on the lowest rung of the gate while he watched her undo Romeo's head collar and set him loose.

Joanna's heart banged at her ribs and she hovered near the horse for as long as she could, prolonging the moment when she'd have to face Seb. Even thinking about the way he'd kissed her made her cheeks flame and her knees tremble.

Damn. She just wasn't used to feeling like this and she didn't know how to handle it. *She didn't know what to say to the man.* Kissing men just wasn't something she did.

She walked across the hard earth to the gate, her eyes avoiding his.

'What are you doing here? You're normally out in the evenings.'

She'd been banking on it.

'I'm going out later.' He straightened and moved to one side so that she could climb over the gate. 'And you're coming with me.'

'Me?' She leapt to the ground and gaped up at him in astonishment.

'Yes, you.' He looked amused and warm colour touched her cheeks.

'Are…' She broke off, strangely hesitant. 'Are you asking me out?'

'Yes.' One dark eyebrow lifted. 'Why is that so surprising?'

'Well, because men never—' She stopped and bit her lip, wishing she would sometimes remember to engage her brain before she spoke.

'Men never what?' His voice was soft, and she gave a sigh and dragged her hat off her head.

'Men never ask me out.' She tried to keep the hurt out of her voice. 'I have it on good authority that I'm not "date" material.'

His mouth tightened and his eyes sparked with an anger that surprised her. 'Who told you that?'

She shrugged and looked away, wondering why he cared. 'Does it matter?'

'Well, at least tell me you didn't believe him!' His tone

was incredulous. 'How did you ever develop such a low opinion of yourself?'

'I haven't got a low opinion of myself. Not really. I'm just realistic.' She looked at him and sighed. 'Oh, come on, Seb, let's just be honest for a minute, shall we? You can date just about any woman on the planet. Why would you want to waste an evening with a boring doctor whose idea of excitement is a night in with a book?'

He winced slightly as she threw his words back at him. 'I was wrong to say that,' he said quietly. 'I know you better now.'

She shook her head. 'You weren't wrong, Seb. You were absolutely right about me. A night in with a book *is* my idea of excitement.'

There was a pause and his eyes gleamed with humour. 'Ah, but that's because you've never been on a date with me.'

A date with Seb…

Joanna tensed, her heart thudding uncontrollably. 'Has anyone ever told you that you're arrogant, Seb?'

'Frequently.' He nodded slowly, his gorgeous eyes still brimming with laughter. 'So now we've cleared that up, will you have dinner with me?'

She raked a hand through her tangled hair, suddenly exasperated. 'No, I won't.'

'Why not?'

There were hundreds of reasons.

'Well, because I've got work to do for a start—'

He tutted and took a step closer to her. 'Oh Joanna, Joanna, remember what happened last time you mentioned work.'

She started to back away. Being so close to him made her feel strange. 'Is that what this is all about? You kissed me so now you think you'd better ask me out?' She didn't know what to say. How to handle him. This type of conversation was totally outside her experience. 'You needn't worry, Seb. Let's just forget it.'

There was a long silence and then she felt his strong fingers lift her chin, forcing her to look at him.

'I've tried that and so far with little success.' His voice was slightly gruff. 'So I thought dinner might give us a chance to talk and get to know each other better.'

The blood pounded in her ears and she jerked away from him. 'I have to go and get changed.' She felt totally confused.

'Fine. I'll wait for you.'

All her doubts and fears showed in her eyes. 'Are you serious? You really want to have dinner with me?'

He frowned slightly. 'Why else would I ask you?'

She swallowed. 'For a joke?'

There was a long silence and then he lifted a finger and touched her cheek gently. 'Someone did treat you badly, didn't they?' His blue eyes searched hers for a long moment. 'Just for the record, I don't make jokes like that. And, yes, I do really want to have dinner with you.'

Her breathing was uneven. 'We hate each other...'

A smile touched his hard mouth. 'You sound like a schoolgirl sometimes, do you know that?'

Although she wasn't about to admit it, she felt like a schoolgirl sometimes, too. Gauche, awkward and dizzy with excitement. She was certainly no match for his level of sophistication.

'I'm going for a shower.' She determinedly turned on her heel.

'Fifteen minutes,' he called after her, his voice firm and very male. 'You have fifteen minutes to get ready or I'm taking you out to dinner as you are.'

She looked back, one eyebrow lifted, her blonde hair tumbling over her shoulders. 'Caveman tactics, Dr Macaulay?'

He grinned. 'Whatever it takes, Dr Weston. Whatever it takes.'

Whatever it takes…

Why on earth was Seb suddenly so determined to have dinner with her? Just because they'd suddenly discovered that they could work together, it didn't mean that they had to socialise. The truth was she didn't want to socialise. Being near him made her feel strange…

Joanna stared gloomily into her wardrobe, realising that there was absolutely nothing in there remotely suitable for dinner with anyone, let alone Seb.

Where was he planning to take her? Somewhere flashy probably.

She tugged out a dress that had been given to her by a grateful patient who had owned a stylish boutique somewhere in the West Country.

She'd never worn it.

It was bright fuchsia and strappy. Summery and frivolous. Not her at all. But ever since Seb had kissed her she wasn't sure who she was any more. Her whole identity had somehow become confused.

She stared at the dress doubtfully then slipped it over her head and wriggled it down over the soft swell of her hips.

With a gasp of shock she realised just how much cleavage the dress showed, but before she could take it off there was a tap on her bedroom door.

'Are you ready?'

'No!' Joanna glanced at her reflection in the mirror in dismay. She looked totally wanton. 'I need more time.'

'I said fifteen minutes—' Seb opened the door and stopped dead, taking in her appearance with one sweep of those eyes. 'Not ready? How much more ready can you get? You look great.'

'This isn't what I'm wearing,' she said hastily, and he lifted an eyebrow.

'It looks as though you're wearing it to me.'

She bit her lip. 'I mean, I was just trying it on—but it doesn't suit me…'

There was a pause while he looked at her, his gaze resting on the low neckline.

'Oh, it suits you, Joanna,' he said softly. 'It really suits you. But that's the problem, isn't it? That dress is plumage, not armour—and you usually wear armour.'

She stared at him in total panic, feeling again as if he were peeling away her privacy layer by layer.

'Let's just forget this, Seb—it isn't going to work.'

'What's not to work? I'm asking you to eat dinner with me,' he pointed out gently. 'How hard can that be?'

Very hard. Her body didn't behave in its normal predictable fashion when she was with him. It was doing something strange that wasn't in any of the textbooks she'd ever read.

'I don't want to eat dinner,' she said firmly, walking briskly across her bedroom and slipping a cardigan over the dress. At least she felt less naked! 'I never go out to dinner.'

'You never went out for lunch until today,' he said reasonably, 'and you enjoyed that.'

She glared at him. 'You gave me no choice about lunch.'

'And I'm giving you no choice about dinner,' he said calmly. 'Caveman tactics, remember? You enjoyed lunch and I'm willing to bet you'll enjoy dinner.'

She hesitated, suddenly uncertain. 'I don't like smart restaurants…'

'Who said anything about smart restaurants?' He gave a faint smile. 'You always misjudge me Joanna.'

Her heart was thundering in her chest but there was something that she wanted to get straight between them.

She took a deep breath. 'And I don't want you to kiss me again, Seb. Is that clear?'

She probably didn't even need to say it. Why would he even want to kiss her again?

'Why?'

Hot colour flooded her cheeks. 'Well, because I—you— we—' She broke off, swallowing hard as he closed the distance between them in two easy strides.

'I enjoyed it, Joanna.' His voice was gentle. 'I can't promise not to do it again.'

He'd enjoyed it?

'It's not what I want, Seb,' she said, twisting her hands together, her chest rising and falling as she struggled to slow her breathing. 'I don't do that sort of thing.'

He gave a faint smile. 'What, like you don't do lunch or dinner? Don't panic, Joanna. Let's just take it a step at a time, OK?'

No, it wasn't OK!

'Seb!'

'Calm down, Joanna.' His voice was deep and steady. 'I can't promise not to kiss you again because frankly it felt fantastic and I'm dying to do it again—but I will promise not to do it without your permission.'

Ignoring her gasp of shock, he grabbed her hand firmly in his and propelled her down the stairs.

As they reached the front door there was a loud hammering and yelling. 'Dr Weston! Dr Weston! Open up. *Help!*'

Seb muttered under his breath. 'Don't these people *ever* give you time off for good behaviour?' He gave a sigh and reached to open the door

A young man stood there, holding a distraught girl in his arms. 'Where's Dr Weston? I need—'

'I'm here,' Joanna said quickly, stepping around Seb and

walking towards the sobbing girl. 'Hello, Mandy. What have you done to yourself?'

'I was chasing him down the road,' Mandy sobbed, her face blotched with tears, 'and my leg just went! And now it's all lumpy and it hurts so much!'

Seb took a quick look. 'She's dislocated her patella,' he said quietly, and Joanna nodded.

'All right, Paul, can you carry her into the surgery? We'll give her some painkillers and deal with it there.'

Paul gave a nod and followed them through the house to the connecting door that led to the surgery.

'Lay her down on the couch, Paul. Seb, let's give her some inhaled nitrous oxide with oxygen to keep her going while we get her something stronger.' Leaving Seb to give the girl Entonox, Joanna walked towards the drugs cabinet, found what she wanted and then walked back to the trolley.

'OK, I'm going to give you some strong painkillers, Mandy. You're not allergic to anything, are you?'

'No.' The girl's breathing was coming in jerks as she cried. 'But I feel really sick. I think I might be sick—'

'Try and take a deep breath for me, Mandy.' Seb moved towards the trolley and took her hand. 'This is soon going to feel better.'

'I'm going to give it into your vein,' Joanna told her, sliding a tourniquet up the girl's arm and tightening it. 'Once it's working, we'll put the patella back into position.'

'You're going to put it back here?' Mandy's eyes flew wide with fright. 'Don't I need an anaesthetic or something?'

'No. Once you've had painkillers we should be able to sort your patella out fairly easily.' Joanna inserted an intravenous cannula and then slowly injected the analgesia into the vein.

'How does that feel now, Mandy?' she asked a few minutes later, and the girl nodded.

'A bit better. But I really don't want you to touch my knee.'

'It's very straightforward,' Seb told her, his voice deep and reassuring as his large hands moved over the girl's leg. 'All we do is straighten the leg—that's it, good girl, just like that. There we are. All done. Simple, wasn't it?'

Mandy stared down at her leg. 'That's it?'

Seb smiled. 'That's it.'

'And will it stay like that or will it happen again?'

'Well, we need to send you into hospital to have it checked by the orthopaedic team,' Seb explained. 'You need an X-ray. We'll just splint it to the other one, using pads and bandages and that will keep it immobile while you go in the ambulance to hospital.'

'Do I really need to go in the ambulance?'

'I'm afraid so.' Seb helped Joanna bandage the affected knee to the other leg. 'We need to keep this leg straight. I'll call the orthopaedic people and warn them that you're on your way.'

The ambulance arrived only minutes later. Seb and Joanna helped the crew load the injured girl into the vehicle and Paul thanked them before climbing in after Mandy.

As the ambulance drew away, Seb turned to Joanna, his eyes gleaming.

'Now then, where were we, Dr Weston…?'

She gave a weak smile. 'You were dragging me out to dinner and I was protesting.'

'That's right, I remember.' He smiled. 'So let's carry on where we left off. Quickly, before any more of your dependants turn up. We're meant to have cover for tonight but obviously I should have asked the out-of-hours doctor to come and live in your house because your patients seem to bypass normal systems and just bang on your door.'

'I'm their doctor,' Joanna pointed out, and his smile widened.

'Not tonight, Dr Weston.' He reached out and stroked her cheek with his fingers. 'Tonight you're my date.'

CHAPTER SIX

His date?

Her heart thumping wildly, Joanna walked with Seb to the car, trying to ignore the cool strength of his fingers as they tightened on hers. Glancing briefly at his handsome profile, she remembered what he'd said about kissing her if she gave permission.

Well, she wasn't going to give him permission, she told herself firmly. The mere thought of kissing him again made her feel odd.

She watched, puzzled, as Seb swung a small rucksack into the boot and slammed it shut.

'Where are we going?'

Why on earth would he be taking a rucksack to dinner?

'Wait and see.' He flashed her a grin that did strange things to her insides and then started the engine and accelerated out of the car park.

Strands of hair whipped around her cheeks and she scooped up her hair and held it in her hand, trying to stop it flying into her eyes.

'Here—borrow my hat.' Seb handed her a black baseball cap which she gratefully pushed down over her wayward blonde curls.

'Thanks.' She squinted at a road sign as they flashed past it. 'We're going to the beach?'

She swivelled in her seat to look at him but he merely shrugged mysteriously, a hint of a smile touching his mouth as he changed gear and eased the car around a tight bend in the road.

Taking advantage of the fact that all his attention was

on the road ahead, Joanna's eyes drifted furtively to his firm mouth, remembering the way he'd kissed her. Despite the warm evening she felt her body shiver with reaction.

Just one kiss.

One kiss—that was all it had taken to turn her from indifferent to aware, from comfortable to confused. One kiss and she was behaving the same way that every other woman behaved around Seb Macaulay.

What had happened to the irritation that she'd always felt towards him? The antipathy? She searched her feelings for a familiar emotion—*something* that she recognised—but there was nothing there that reassured her. Only a kind of breathless excitement, a childish thrill that hadn't been there before and that she didn't understand.

Joanna frowned slightly as she tried to analyse what was happening to her. She'd never been remotely affected by Seb's attractions until now, but suddenly she was noticing all the things that other women had doubtless noticed for years. The way his long, dark lashes partially shielded his very sexy eyes, his sharp blue gaze, his fabulous bone structure and the way his hard jaw was permanently darkened by a tantalising hint of stubble which simply accentuated his masculinity. And his mouth...

It was no wonder women found him irresistible, she thought, dragging her eyes away from his profile and staring at the countryside. She'd never been able to understand it before, but since he'd kissed her everything had changed. Suddenly she was seeing him differently. Which was ridiculous, she told herself stoutly, because, handsome or not, he was still the same frivolous playboy that he'd always been. Someone whose values were totally opposed to her own.

'You're quiet.' He glanced briefly in her direction and she gave him a weak smile, wondering what he'd say if he knew what she was thinking. He'd probably die of shock.

Joanna Weston thinking of something other than work. And
not just something—someone. *Him.*

'I was just wondering where we were going for dinner,'
she lied, and then gave a gasp of pleasure as he turned a
corner and the sea came into view. 'Oh, Seb! It's beautiful.'

The evening sunlight sent shimmering lights across the
surface of the water and she could hear the rhythmic crash
of waves as the tide moved relentlessly towards the tow-
ering cliffs.

He parked in a small car park at the top of the cliffs and
looked at her curiously. 'Are you seriously telling me that
you've been living in this part of the world for three years
and you've never visited this place?'

She hesitated. 'I've been working hard—'

Immediately he lifted a hand and covered her mouth with
his fingers. 'That word is banned this evening. No "work"
and no "buts". OK?'

He climbed out of the car and retrieved his rucksack
from the boot before opening her door to help her out.

She glanced around the empty car park, confused. 'It
doesn't look as though there's a restaurant here.'

'Who said anything about a restaurant?' He smiled at her
and shrugged the rucksack onto his broad shoulders. 'I said
dinner. I didn't say where. Come on. Let's walk.'

Without giving her time to question him further, he
walked off in the direction of the cliff path and by the time
she'd caught up with him she was breathless.

'You should have told me we were walking. I would
have dressed differently.'

'I know.' He glanced towards her with a grin that melted
her bones. 'That's why I didn't tell you. That dress is too
good to spend its life in the back of a wardrobe.'

Totally unused to compliments, she blushed deeply but
he was striding ahead again, so comfortable and relaxed
that Joanna felt herself start to relax, too. She should prob-

ably be relieved, she told herself firmly. She'd feared a starchy restaurant with waiters hovering and instead she'd been given a fabulous walk with wonderful views.

'This looks a good place.' Seb swung the rucksack off his broad shoulders and dropped it to the ground.

Joanna could only stare in surprise as he delved inside and pulled out a blanket. 'Were you a Scout?'

'Well, I'm always prepared if that's what you mean.' He winked at her and waved a hand at the blanket. 'Your table is ready, madam.'

She smiled in spite of herself and knelt down on the blanket, slipping off her shoes and curling her slim legs underneath her.

'This is wonderful.' she murmured softly. 'What a great idea. A picnic.'

'Well, don't get too excited. The food is fairly boring, I'm afraid,' he confessed ruefully, pulling some packages out of the rucksack. 'I hope you like smoked salmon.'

'Love it.' She watched in astonishment as he unwrapped the sandwiches and uncorked a bottle of chilled white wine.

Sandwiches?

Somehow she hadn't associated Seb with sandwiches, even if they were smoked salmon.

He handed her a brimming glass. 'What's the matter?'

She blushed, embarrassed by her own thoughts. 'I just wouldn't have thought this was your ideal place for dinner,' she confessed, deciding that she may as well be honest.

'Ah…' He lifted his glass in a silent toast and took a mouthful of wine. 'But that's because you don't know me, Joanna, just as I don't really know you. But I'm working on it.'

Heat spread though her veins and she glanced away from his penetrating gaze.

'There's nothing to know,' she said quickly, helping herself to a sandwich and looking out over the bay. 'I work,

I own a horse—I lead a very normal life. Especially in comparison to someone like you. I don't go on cruises to exotic locations.'

He leaned forward to take a sandwich. 'It really bothers you, doesn't it,' he said slowly, 'the fact that I haven't settled into the accepted pattern of practising medicine? You think I'm just playing at being a doctor, don't you?'

She shifted slightly, uncomfortably aware that that was exactly what she *did* think.

'I suppose everyone's different,' she conceded finally, giving him a hesitant smile. 'Maybe you're the sort of person who could never be tied down to one place or one job.'

Or one woman.

'Well, you're right in a way,' he murmured, topping up her glass and pushing the sandwiches towards her. 'I do like variety. But I can assure you that my talents aren't wasted.'

Being a doctor to rich, pampered tourists in exotic locations where he could top up his tan? Was that the value he put on his skills?

Still, she didn't want to argue with him. Not this evening, when the sun was warming her exposed limbs and the sea was whispering soothingly at the bottom of the cliffs.

'What about you, Joanna?' He lay back on the rug and closed his eyes with a long sigh of satisfaction. 'Tell me about your family—your background—'

'There's nothing to tell,' she muttered self-consciously, wondering what there was about her life that Seb could possibly be interested in.

'OK, then.' He turned his head and regarded her lazily. 'If you won't volunteer anything, I'll ask questions. Any brothers or sisters?'

'No.' She gave a wistful smile and instantly his eyes narrowed.

'But you would have liked to have had a sibling?'

She glanced at him and then looked back at the sea. 'Yes. I used to dream about it.'

Seb lifted himself on his elbows and watched her closely. 'Why?'

She hesitated, unused to confiding in anyone. 'Because it would have taken the pressure off me,' she said finally, her voice so soft that she wondered whether he would be able to hear her.

'Pressure? From your parents presumably?'

His hearing was obviously as acute as all his other senses.

'Yes.'

'Are they doctors, too?'

'No.' Joanna shook her head vigorously and then stuffed a wayward strand of hair back inside the baseball cap he'd lent her. 'My father was a vicar but both my parents died a few years ago.'

'I'm sorry.' His quiet voice penetrated her thoughts and she turned with a brief smile.

'Don't be. They had me very late in life. In fact, my father told me once that my mother was advised to have a termination because they said that the risks to her health were too great at her age. Naturally she refused. A termination would have been going against everything they believed in so my parents wouldn't even entertain the thought. And anyway they were delighted. They'd always wanted a child but had just assumed that it was never going to happen.'

'So they had you in the autumn of their lives.' Seb said thoughtfully. 'They must have loved you very much.'

'Yes.' She opened her mouth to say more and then closed it again. Why was she even considering confiding in this man she didn't really know? Was one kiss all it took for her to lose her sense of judgement?

'And with the weight of their love came the weight of

expectation,' he murmured, his eyes never leaving her face. 'Is that why you always studied so hard?'

She stared at him, stunned that he could be so acute. 'Yes. At first anyway. My parents wanted me to have a good career.'

'So they piled all their expectations on you.' Seb sat up and helped himself to another sandwich. 'It must have been tough, being a vicar's daughter.'

Joanna gazed into her glass of wine. 'Well, let's just say it didn't take me long to realise that I was different from everyone else.'

'Different?' He took a mouthful of sandwich and frowned slightly. 'In what way were you different?'

She was silent, her mind wandering painfully back to those years of childhood isolation.

'I wasn't allowed to do any of the things that the other girls did so it was almost impossible to build a friendship. And because I couldn't join in, I was teased.'

He paused with the sandwich halfway to his mouth. 'Teased or bullied?'

She glanced across the bay and swallowed hard. 'Bullied,' she admitted finally. 'Hardly surprising really. I never fitted in. When the other girls all met up on a Saturday to experiment with make-up and giggle about boys, I was at home, studying.'

'But surely your parents must have let you see friends?'

'Not really. The girls I wanted to be friends with were ''unsuitable'', according to my father. He thought that make-up and clothes were the trappings of sin. All he wanted me to do was study.'

'And your mother?'

'She would never have disagreed with my father,' Joanna said quietly. 'She wanted me to work hard, too, and in the end that's what I did. I suppose, if I'm honest, I saw work as a kind of escape although, of course, it made things worse at school.'

'Because you were seen as a swot?'

'Yes. It just made me even more different from the rest of my peer group.' She gave a shrug and struggled to produce a smile. 'But I survived.'

Seb let out a long breath. 'You must have been glad to leave school.'

'Yes.' She nodded slowly. 'I thought that medical school would be a fresh start.'

He was watching her intently. 'But it wasn't?'

'No.' She shook her head. 'Only this time it was nobody's fault but my own. I'd spent so long in my own company, trying to avoid being noticed and bullied, that I'd totally lost the ability to socialise. I was painfully shy with people. I suppose the truth is that I didn't really know how to make friends because I'd never really had any.'

'You're a very pretty girl, Joanna,' he said softly. 'I can't believe that men didn't show an interest in you.'

Deciding that she'd said more than enough, she scrambled hastily to her feet.

'That's enough about me. Let's walk while it's still light.'

'It's only seven o'clock,' he pointed out gently. 'It's going to be light for hours yet. And you haven't finished your story yet. Sit down and tell me what happened.'

She wrapped her arms around her waist and turned to him, her eyes wide. 'What makes you think anything happened?'

'Because of the way you're reacting,' he said gruffly. 'Because of the way you've locked so much of yourself away. It's obvious. And I wish you'd tell me the whole story. It might make you feel better.'

Make her feel better? To share her humiliation with him? Hardly!

'There's nothing to tell,' she mumbled, bending down to pick up her shoes. Seb's long, strong fingers clamped round her wrist and he pulled her gently back onto the rug.

'Is he the reason you still work so hard?' His voice was low and urgent. 'Is he the reason you don't seem to have a social life?'

Joanna stared at him. 'Is who the reason?'

His gaze held hers steadily. 'The louse who obviously took advantage of your naïvety.'

She coloured hotly and tried to jerk her wrist away, but his grip tightened. 'I really don't want to talk about this, Seb.'

He frowned thoughtfully. 'I know our paths didn't cross that much but I don't ever remember you with a boyfriend.'

She struggled for a moment, physically and mentally, and then she gave in to the sympathy and kindness she saw in his eyes.

'It was at the beginning,' she mumbled, her slim shoulders sagging as she sat down next to him again. 'I met him in freshers' week.'

'Your very first week away from home?'

She nodded slowly. 'Yes. I went to a disco in the medics' bar and he—I—' She broke off, embarrassed by how totally naïve and stupid she'd been. 'Let's just say he was really attractive and he was the first man who'd ever paid me any attention.'

'I can imagine how that must have felt,' Seb said quietly, his gaze sympathetic. 'After eighteen years of being over-protected by your parents, freshers' week must have seemed like a free run in a sweet shop.'

She gave him a half-smile, surprised and grateful that he seemed to understand how strange it had all been to her.

'Don't tell me.' He gave a humourless laugh. 'You spent the night with him and he never called you again.'

If only that had been the way it had happened…

She shook her head blindly, taken by surprise as the tears filled her eyes, Damn. What an idiot. Crying after all these years.

She cleared her throat and jumped to her feet again, only this time, instead of pulling her down again, he stood up, too, and turned her to face him.

'Why am I getting such a bad feeling about this?' he asked grimly. 'What the hell happened, Joanna?'

She took a deep breath. 'Well, let's just say he wasn't an innocent stranger after all. It turned out that he was the cousin of one of the boys that I'd been to school with— one of the bullies. I didn't know that at the time. I was stupid enough to think that he was genuinely interested in me. It wasn't until we'd been going out for a month, until after he'd said that he loved me and finally got me to go to bed with him, that I found the photograph and the letter.'

'Go on.' Seb's biting tone startled Joanna and her eyes flew to his as she finished her story.

'It had been a bet, of course,' she said dully. 'The letter said, "A photograph of the vicar's daughter naked and in my bed to prove that you owe me £1000."' She swallowed painfully and looked away, missing the flash of undiluted fury in Seb's eyes. 'The high price my school tormentor placed on me just underlined how totally unlikely he thought it that anyone would ever want to go to bed with me. Afterwards I found out that his cousin had a reputation as a womaniser and he could have charmed the birds from the trees.'

'And that was it? That was the end of your relationship?'

'There wasn't a relationship, Seb. He never really wanted me. And just to prove it he pinned the photograph and the letter to the noticeboard—I'm surprised you never saw it.'

There was a long silence and when Joanna finally plucked up the courage to look at him she saw that his eyes were cold with anger.

'Who was he?' Seb's voice was strangely flat, and she gave a shrug.

'What does it matter?'

Seb's mouth tightened. 'Who, Joanna?'

'Charlie Wellingford,' she muttered, unable to say his name without feeling angry with herself. Even now, after all these years, she couldn't forgive herself for having been taken in by him. How could she have been so stupid?

Seb gave a harsh laugh. 'Wellingford—I suppose I should have guessed.'

'Did you know him?'

Seb shrugged. 'Not very well, but well enough to know that he was a complete jerk and a menace to women.' His voice softened and he lifted her chin with his fingers, forcing her to look at him. 'But on the surface he was glamorous, wealthy and handsome, and I can see exactly why he would have been irresistible to someone from your background.'

Joanna bit her lip. 'There's more…'

Having got this far, she may as well confess the whole, sorry story.

Seb's jaw tensed. 'Go on.'

'After he pinned the photo to the noticeboard I found out that I was pregnant.' Her throat thickened and she swallowed hard. 'I was so scared, Seb.'

He gave a groan and folded her in his arms. 'You poor thing. What did you do?'

'Nothing.' For a brief moment Joanna leaned her head against his hard chest, his tantalising male scent making her senses swim. 'It took care of itself. I had a miscarriage. I suppose I should have been relieved really, but I wasn't. I just felt devastated.'

Seb swore softly and hugged her tighter. 'I'm sorry.'

His warmth and strength was too much to take. She was going to make a fool of herself.

Joanna pulled away quickly. 'I should have known better.'

'Why?' His voice was gruff. 'You were little more than a child. Did you ever tell your parents?'

'Are you joking?' She shook her head. 'They would have died of mortification. Their only daughter pregnant at the age of eighteen—no, I didn't tell them Seb. I didn't tell anyone.'

He breathed out sharply. 'But who supported you? Who looked after you?'

'No one.' She gave a painful smile. 'I buried myself in my work and eventually everything started to hurt less.'

Seb muttered something under his breath. 'I want you to tell me that you found a nice normal man to restore your faith in human nature, but I have a feeling that you didn't. Am I right?'

She gave a wan smile and nodded slowly. 'Yes. I didn't have much confidence anyway and Charlie destroyed the little I had. A few men asked me out but only because I was different.'

Seb frowned. 'How do you know that was why they asked you out?'

'Because it was obvious,' she muttered, embarrassed by the turn of the discussion. 'I'm not the sort of woman that men fall for. Charlie made that clear enough. He would never have gone near me if his cousin hadn't challenged him with the bet. I'm not like most women. I never say the right things and I don't know how to flirt.'

'How refreshing,' Seb drawled, closing the gap between them until their bodies were touching again. 'Has it ever occurred to you that men might ask you out because you're a nice person and very pretty?'

Pretty?

'You're being ridiculous,' she mumbled, trying to move away from him. 'I'm not pretty.'

'Try polishing your mirror,' he countered softly. 'You're very pretty. Especially when you let your hair down. That day I saw you with Romeo, I couldn't believe it was you. I almost fell over with shock.'

Joanna's eyes widened. He'd been staring at her hair because he liked it? Not because it had looked a mess?

'I've worn it like that since I had my interview at medical school,' she confessed. 'My father said that no one would take a woman with long blonde hair seriously so I'd better hide it or cut it off.'

'Well thank goodness you didn't cut it off,' Seb muttered, running his long fingers through the blonde curls and anchoring her head with his hands. 'And stop scraping it back. I promise to take you seriously even if your hair is loose.'

She stared up at him, her heart pounding. Part of her wanted him to kiss her again but part of her knew it was ridiculous. That she was risking making a fool of herself again by falling for the wrong type of man. What did a woman like her have to offer a man like Seb who could have just about anything or anyone he wanted?

His hot gaze collided with hers and her heart thudded slowly as he drew her against him and lowered his head.

'No!' She looked at his mouth, her heart thumping. 'You can't. We mustn't. You promised—'

'No, I didn't.' His voice was low and unbelievably sexy. 'I promised not to kiss you without your permission.'

'Well, then...' Her voice was a hoarse whisper as she felt him draw her closer still.

'So give me permission, Joanna,' he murmured softly against her mouth. 'Quickly. Before I break a promise for the first time in my life.'

She was shivering in his arms. 'I don't believe you really want to kiss me...'

His gaze was suddenly intent. 'I've already told you that I don't play those sorts of games, Joanna.'

'Seb...'

'"Kiss me, Seb",' he muttered, 'that's all you have to say. "Kiss me, Seb."'

She should have pushed him away, should have said nothing, but instead her lips formed the words he wanted and immediately his mouth fused with hers.

He kissed her slowly and thoroughly and then with a low groan he dragged her hips against his, settling her against the growing hardness of his arousal.

Joanna was trembling like a drenched kitten, her body on fire with a need she couldn't identify. All she knew was that she needed more of him. More of the way he tasted. More of the way he touched her...

A cheeky wolf whistle swiftly quenched the heat that was building between them, and Seb lifted his head reluctantly, muttering under his breath as he watched the group of Scouts trooping along the beach below them.

'Oops.' He turned back to her with a wry smile and bent his head again, but she pushed at his chest and stumbled away from him, her body still burning with the feelings he'd aroused.

'No, Seb.'

'Why "no"?'

'Because it's crazy,' she said desperately, backing further along the path to put a safe distance between them. She didn't trust herself.

'And why is it crazy?' His voice was firm but conversational, and she bit her lip hard.

'Because there's no reason for you to kiss me.'

'I thought we'd already established that I want to. As far as I'm concerned, that's a good enough reason.' He moved towards her slowly. 'Providing you want to as well—and you gave me permission, remember. You wanted it, too, Joanna.'

She had. Oh, dear heaven, she had. But that want—*that need*—wasn't enough to make her blind to the reality of their situations. He was totally the wrong sort of man for her. She needed someone more serious—she could never really accept his careless attitude to life.

'Not long ago we were arguing,' she reminded him, desperate to cool the flames that were still flickering between them. 'We couldn't stand the sight of each other.'

'Which just goes to show how wrong people can be,' he said evenly, stopping directly in front of her and staring down into her pale face with a frown.

'W-we have nothing in common,' she stammered, and he smiled.

'I disagree. We complement each other surprisingly well.' He ran a finger gently over her cheek. 'Or at least we would if you stopped making assumptions about me. Why don't you just trust me, Joanna?'

'Because I've done that once before,' she said simply. 'Deluded myself into thinking that someone found me attractive. But I was wrong.'

He gave her a look that was half amused and half exasperated. 'Are you saying that you think I faked my reaction to you a minute ago?'

She remembered the hard ridge of pressure against her and coloured deeply. 'No, but...'

He waited for her to say more and then sighed. 'OK.' He lifted his hands and cupped her face in his, forcing her to look at him. 'We'll leave it for now. I understand it must be hard for you to trust anyone. But start looking more closely in your mirror. You, Joanna Weston, are a very attractive woman. Very attractive. Yes, you annoy the hell out of me and make me blazingly angry but I want you more than any woman I've ever met.'

With that he released her and bent to pack the picnic rug back in the rucksack, leaving her to digest his words in stunned silence.

He thought she was very attractive?

He wanted her more than any woman he'd ever met?

Joanna watched, numb with shock, as he swung the rucksack onto his shoulders and then turned to her with an easy smile.

'Come on, Dr Weston, let's go for a walk before you think of more reasons why you couldn't possibly have a wild affair with me.'

He strode off along the coast path and she stood staring after him, glued to the spot by his parting words.

A wild affair?

Was that what he was proposing?

Just the thought of a wild affair with him made her limbs tremble and her lungs gasp for air.

What would it be like to have an affair with a man like Seb?

She shook herself mentally, shocked by her own thoughts. Never in her life before—*never*—had she ever been tempted to have an affair. She'd only slept with Charlie because he'd said that he loved her and—little more than a child—she'd believed him. She just wasn't interested in affairs and she never had been. Affairs were about sex and sex wasn't important to her. She wasn't like other women.

Was she?

CHAPTER SEVEN

AFTER the evening on the cliff, even being within the same building as Seb made Joanna jumpy.

Just the sound of his voice in the distance was enough to make her pulse race, and the sight of those broad shoulders over the breakfast table made her knees tremble.

And he knew it…

She might be naïve about men and relationships but she sensed that he was skillfully wearing down her defences. He never did more than kiss her but each time he did that he seemed to take it a stage further, cranking up the heat between them until she thought her body might explode.

She was amazed that Laura hadn't noticed a change between them but somehow they seemed to manage to go about their work as if nothing had changed.

Little Elliot Hunt made a surprisingly rapid recovery and when Joanna called the hospital she was told that he'd made remarkable progress and should be discharged in a few days.

'He's a lucky little boy,' Seb said when she told him the news, and she nodded.

'Yes. If his mother hadn't called when she did or you hadn't taken the decision to give him that penicillin…' She broke off, hardly able to think about the alternative scenario.

'Dr Weston?' Laura put her head round the door of the consulting room, her pretty face creased with worry. 'I've got one of the community midwives on the phone. They want to speak to you about Ruth Kenton.'

Joanna exchanged glances with Seb and quickly picked up the phone. 'Dr Weston speaking.'

She listened as the midwife outlined the problem then nodded swiftly. 'It sounds as though she needs to be admitted, doesn't it? You make the arrangements at your end and I'll speak to the hospital. Tell Ruth I'll come and see her in the unit this afternoon when I've finished my calls.'

She replaced the receiver and dialled again, this time calling the hospital to warn the obstetric consultant that Ruth was on her way in.

'Problems?' Seb's tone was quiet as she finally replaced the receiver.

She gave a slow nod. 'Possibly. Helen, our community midwife, visited her this morning and said that Ruth's blood pressure has shot up and she has significant protein in her urine.'

'Well, she's lucky that she's been able to stay at home for as long as she has,' Seb pointed out, and she gave him a tired smile.

'I suppose so, although I can't imagine how they'll manage if she's in hospital for weeks.'

There was another tap on the door and Laura popped her head round again, obviously embarrassed to be disturbing them again.

'I'm sorry, Dr Weston. I've got Tim Peters in Reception—'

Joanna frowned, baffled. 'Tim Peters?'

'Vera and John's son,' Laura told her, and Joanna's face cleared.

'Oh, yes, I remember them telling me about him, although I've never met him.'

What could he possibly want? Was he concerned about his parents?

'He wanted to see you but you've got a full list,' Laura told her, obviously unsure as to what to do.

'Give me two of Dr Weston's patients,' Seb suggested quickly, 'unless they've specifically asked to see her. That should free up time for you to talk to him.'

Joanna looked at him doubtfully. 'Are you sure?'

'Of course.' He smiled. 'We both want to get to the bottom of what's going on in that household, and who better to shed light on the problem than the son?'

It made sense and Joanna gave a nod. 'All right, then, thank you. Laura, do as Dr Macaulay suggests and shift a couple of patients so that we can slot Tim in.'

Tim was a thin, anxious-looking man in his mid-thirties who was obviously extremely worried about his parents.

'You must think I'm really odd, coming to you like this,' he apologised as he settled himself in the chair by Joanna's desk, 'but I really didn't know what else to do.'

'It's no problem at all.' Joanna reassured him immediately, and gave him a warm smile. 'Why don't you tell me what's worrying you?'

She had a strong suspicion what was worrying him, of course, but she wanted to hear him tell her himself.

He shifted awkwardly in his seat, clearly uncomfortable about talking to her. 'I feel totally disloyal saying this to you behind their backs, but it's my parents...'

'Go on.'

'Well, to be precise, it's my mum,' he said simply, shrugging his shoulders in a helpless gesture. 'She's just not herself. She's changed.'

Joanna leaned forward. 'In what way has she changed?'

'My parents have been married for forty years,' Tim told her, 'and lately she's been awful to my dad. Shouting at him, swearing—awful swearing. I've never heard my mother swear in her life before. And then last Saturday she hit him.'

'She hit him?'

Tim nodded. 'With his old cricket bat. She said that if

he insisted on spending the entire weekend playing cricket then he had it coming. Trouble is, Dad's got arthritis, as you know, and he struggles to walk to the local shop let alone play cricket. He hasn't played a game of cricket for at least fifteen years.'

Joanna sat back in her chair. 'How often do you see them, Tim?'

'Every few weeks. A bit less lately, to be honest, because of the rows, but it didn't occur to me at first that something was wrong.' He frowned and rubbed a hand over the back of his neck to relieve the pressure. 'I thought they were just getting on each other's nerves, as any couple do sometimes.'

Joanna nodded sympathetically. 'Are they looking after themselves properly, do you think?'

'Well, they seem to eat all right,' Tim said slowly. 'Mum gets a lift to the shops from her neighbour so there's always plenty of food in the house. The problem is more the way she behaves, if you know what I mean. It's as if she'd had a complete personality change. And she wanders around at night, which is a real worry.'

'Do they know that you've come to see me today?' Joanna's tone was gentle and Tim shook his head vigorously.

'No! And, frankly, I don't think I'd want to tell them— well, not my mother anyway. She'd wouldn't thank me for interfering and she's so moody these days.'

'And she hasn't always been moody?' Joanna was keen to clarify the old woman's previous behaviour.

'My mum?' Tim sighed despondently. 'No. She was the sweetest, most gentle person around. Ask anyone in this village. That's why I can't understand it. She just isn't herself any more, Dr Weston.'

'Thank you for coming to see me, Tim,' Joanna said quietly. 'You did the right thing. What I need to do now

is talk to both your parents and run some tests. There could
be several things that could cause the problems that you're
describing. Is there any chance that you could be at home
when I call?'

Tim looked dubious. 'Would that help?'

'I think it might,' Joanna said. 'What about this afternoon? I could call round to see how they are and assess
the situation then.'

'All right.' Tim nodded and stood up. 'Thanks, Dr
Weston.'

Joanna walked with him to the door. 'I'll see you around
lunchtime, Tim.'

She watched him go with a sinking heart. It was always
possible that John had pushed Vera to breaking point and
she was losing her temper, but it sounded more as though
the old lady was displaying signs of dementia or an acute
confusional state.

She worked her way steadily through her morning list
and then walked through to Reception, noticing that there
was only one patient in the waiting room—a young girl in
a wheelchair.

Joanna checked the computer. 'Is she waiting to see a
doctor?'

Laura nodded. 'Dr Macaulay.'

'I'll see her,' Joanna said immediately. 'Dr Macaulay
saw several of my patients this morning so it's the least I
can do.'

Laura shook her head, her expression mysterious. 'I
don't think she wants medical help. I think she just wants
to see Dr Macaulay. You know—as a friend.'

'Oh.' Joanna was slightly taken aback but at that moment
the door to Seb's consulting room opened and he strolled
out, laughing with his patient as they walked into
Reception. And then he saw the young girl in the wheelchair and stopped in surprise.

'Letty?' Astonishment turned to delight and he crossed the room in three long strides and bent to give the child an enormous hug. 'What a surprise! What are you doing here?'

'I'm visiting Gabby,' the girl told him, reaching up again to give him a big hug. 'She told me you were here. I wanted to come and see you to thank you for everything you did.'

'Silly child.' Seb's tone was gruff and he was clearly moved by the girl's presence. 'So how have you been?'

'Oh, you know how it is…' She gave a cheerful smile and a shrug that spoke volumes. 'Up and down. My leg's been pretty sore but the surgeon says that it should settle down eventually. Oh, and, Dr Macaulay, I've started riding!'

Seb gave a lopsided smile. 'Good girl. I always said you could do it.'

'I know you did.' Letty's voice was soft. 'But I didn't believe you. Not at first. It seemed like a dream. A fantasy. I would have given up if it hadn't been for you.'

Seb touched her cheek gently. 'No you wouldn't. You're a fighter, Letty.'

She shook her head. 'No. You gave me the courage to go on.' Suddenly she glanced around guiltily. 'Sorry. I forgot you were working. Am I disturbing you, visiting like this without warning you first?'

Seb shook his head and glanced at Joanna who was hovering discreetly in the background.

'This is Dr Weston, my partner. Joanna, this brave little girl is Letty Thomas.'

'Hello.' Joanna gave the girl a warm smile. 'So this is a personal visit, not a professional one.'

Letty nodded and then glanced adoringly at Seb. 'I wanted to see him. He changed my life totally and I wanted to say thank you.' She blushed slightly. 'I should have said it at the time but I was so angry and bitter and wrapped up in myself I couldn't see what he was doing.'

What was she talking about?

Joanna frowned, puzzled. 'Were you a patient of Seb's?'

'No.' Letty shook her head. 'Well, not exactly. He was the doctor on the cruise they sent me on.'

Cruise? Letty had been on the cruise? What sort of a cruise had it been?

Joanna turned to Seb, her eyes questioning, but he merely shrugged and looked embarrassed.

'He saved my life,' Letty said simply. 'I lost my leg, you see. In an accident. I didn't see the point of living. But my doctor knew about this charity that sends disabled children on special holidays and that was where I met Seb.'

On a holiday for disabled children? Not a cruise for the rich and pampered...

'Sebastian?' She turned to look at him, her gaze accusing and embarrassed. She'd misjudged him again. Written him off as a party animal who treated work as a frivolity. Yet here was this girl saying that he'd been helping disabled children.

'It was just a job, Joanna,' he said quickly, sliding a finger round the collar of his shirt as if it were too tight. 'Just a job.'

'He's lying,' Letty said calmly. 'He's always like that. Really modest. He doesn't tell you that he stayed up one entire night with me while I was crying, helping me to see that I could rebuild my life. And I wasn't the only one he helped. He taught little Eva to swim and she'd been too terrified to go near water since her accident, and Peter had been blind—'

'Yes, OK, Letty,' Seb interrupted her quickly, clearly uncomfortable. 'I'm sure Dr Weston doesn't want to know the details.'

'Actually, I do,' Joanna said softly. 'I really, really do.'

She settled herself in the chair next to Letty, ignoring Seb's embarrassed protest, and listened while the girl told her everything about the charity and how it had changed her life.

'And was Seb the only doctor?'

'No.' Letty shook her head. 'There were lots of staff so that the children had as much attention as they needed, but he was the boss, of course.'

Of course?

Since when had Seb taken that degree of responsibility for anything? Had she really misjudged him so badly?

Joanna rubbed shaking fingers along her brow and took a deep breath, her thoughts tangled.

'I've got to go,' she said finally, standing up and giving a regretful smile. 'I've got calls to do. It was really great to meet you, Letty, and if you're not in a hurry I hope you'll stay for lunch. Why don't you go through to the house, Seb, and have lunch together?'

He gave a sharp frown. 'I've got calls to do, too.'

'Only three,' Joanna told him quickly, 'I checked with Laura. I'll do those, Seb. You spend some time with Letty.'

'All right, if you're sure.' He was watching her closely but she looked away quickly, unable to meet his eyes, totally confused by exactly who this man was. She'd thought she'd known who he was—what sort of person he was— but she was rapidly discovering that she'd been completely wrong in her assessment of him.

Instead of being a fun-seeking playboy, Letty had shown her that he was a warm, dedicated doctor with a strong need to help others.

And her reasons for not allowing herself to get involved with him were rapidly crumbling into the dust.

Vera and John Peters lived in a small terraced cottage on the outskirts of the village, and as she tapped on their front door Joanna felt a flicker of trepidation. What sort of reception would she get from them?

John opened the door, his expression surprised when he saw who their caller was.

'Dr Weston? How nice to see you, my dear. What can we do for you?'

'I was just in the area,' Joanna said quickly, 'and I thought I'd call to see how you both are. Vera had a few problems with her skin when she saw me last.'

'You want to see Vera?' A look of panic flickered across his face. 'She's not feeling too good today...'

'All the more reason for me to see her,' Joanna said gently. 'I'm her doctor, Mr Peters.'

'Of course you are.' He gave a wan smile, hesitated a moment longer and then stood aside, shaking his head slowly. 'She isn't herself, Doctor, she isn't herself.'

'Then let me talk to her.' Joanna squeezed his arm to reassure him as she walked into the house. 'We need to sort this out, Mr Peters.'

John nodded slowly and gestured towards the sitting room. 'Go on through, Doctor. She's in there with our son Tim. He's here on a visit.'

Vera was sitting in a chair by the empty fireplace, rocking slightly and staring at nothing in particular.

'Mum?' Tim glanced at Joanna and then back at his mother. 'There's someone to see you.'

Vera looked up and her face blackened. 'I've told you before not to bring your tarts into this house, Tim Peters!!'

Tim went red and he gave Joanna an agonised look. 'Mum, it's Dr Weston, remember?'

'Dr Weston?' Vera frowned. 'I don't know a Dr Weston. I've had Dr Mills for forty years. Where's Dr Mills?'

'He's in Australia, Mrs Peters,' Joanna said quietly, walking across the room and crouching down next to the old lady. 'I'm his partner and I've come to see you today because I was worried about you.'

Vera glared at her. 'I suppose you're trying to get your scheming hands on my son!'

'Mum, please!'

'It doesn't matter, Tim,' Joanna said softly, quick to reassure the mortified man that she wasn't in the least offended by his mother's comments. On the contrary, she was sad. Very sad. Because she could see for herself that Vera was very different from the old lady she'd seen occasionally over the past three years.

'She's been like this for months.' John spoke at last, his tone so tired and defeated that Joanna felt her heart melt. 'I suppose I should have told someone sooner, but I kept hoping she'd wake up one morning and be all right.'

Joanna stood up and followed him into the kitchen, waiting silently as he filled the kettle.

'When you've been married to someone for forty years, it's difficult to admit that they're confused,' he said, his quiet dignity bringing a lump to Joanna's throat. 'And it's even harder to admit it to other people.'

So John had known for a long time and had been protecting his beloved wife.

Joanna swallowed hard. That was real love…

Pulling herself together, she forced herself to get on with the practicalities, assessing the home situation and whether the old lady was really a danger to her husband.

'I'll need to run some tests, Mr Peters,' she said quietly. 'I want to rule out certain medical problems.'

'It's dementia,' John said flatly, switching off the kettle and pouring the water into a teapot. 'I knew it from the first, although I didn't admit it even to myself. Her mother had it, you know, and her older sister…'

'We'll still run some tests,' Joanna said gently, knowing in her heart that he was right and that the outcome was likely to be dementia.

An hour later she left the house and felt emotionally

drained as she finished her house calls and then drove the thirty miles to the hospital.

The first person she saw was Sue Hunt, Elliot's mother, who was pressing money into a machine to try and get herself a coffee. Her face lit up when she saw Joanna.

'Oh, Dr Weston, it's so good to see you.' Her eyes began to fill with tears of relief but she managed to hold them back. 'He's going to be all right, you know. The doctors say he's on the mend and shouldn't have any complications.'

'I'm glad.' Joanna gave her shoulders a squeeze and they talked for a bit longer before Joanna made her excuses and took the stairs up to the maternity unit on the third floor.

She found Ruth Kenton's bed empty and hurried to the sister's office.

'I'm Dr Weston, Ruth's GP—' she began, but the older woman gave her a warm smile.

'They sectioned her this morning. They decided that the baby was better out than in. Last thing I heard it was doing very well on special care. A little on the small side but breathing without oxygen and surprisingly fit in the circumstances.'

'The scan was suspicious,' Joanna said, and the woman nodded.

'I read that in the notes but the paediatrician says that the baby seems fine apart from being small.'

'And Ruth?'

'They're waiting for her blood pressure to settle but she's doing well. She should be back on the ward in the next few minutes.'

Joanna spent half an hour with an elated Ruth and her husband Tom and then drove slowly back to the surgery, wondering whether Letty would still be there.

She wasn't, but Laura was, clutching a newspaper clipping, her eyes as wide as saucers.

'Look at this…'

Joanna took the clipping, her mouth drying as she saw the picture.

It was Seb, but not as she'd ever seen him before. Gone were the expensively cut trousers and shirts, the smooth dark hair and the laughing eyes. The man in the picture was so filthy and covered in dust that his mode of dress was completely unidentifiable. A battered hard hat was crammed down onto his head and his face was streaked with dirt.

And he was carrying a child….

Joanna swallowed as she read the caption. 'Dr Dare—an unidentified British doctor risks his life to save a child from a collapsing building after the devastating earthquake that hit…'

She stopped reading and looked up, her expression blank. Earthquake?

'Where did you get this, Laura?'

'From Letty, that girl that came to see him earlier. Seb asked me to keep her company while he took a phone call, and she pulled this out of her pocket and showed me. Imagine him not telling anyone that it was him.' Laura bit her lip. 'Letty said that Seb hates people knowing and that he never told anyone he was there. Apparently she found out by accident from one of the people that ran the disabled holiday that she went on with him.'

Joanna stared down at the newspaper clipping, torn apart with guilt as she remembered the things she'd said to him. She'd accused him of being frivolous—of wasting his medical training.

Dear God, how could she have been so stupid? She gave a groan and covered her eyes with her hand.

How could she not have seen the signs?

He was such a good, dedicated doctor, she should have

guessed that he would have been doing something worthwhile. But she'd been so quick to condemn him.

Too quick.

Far from being the playboy she'd accused him of being, the man was a hero. And a modest hero at that. He'd never once mentioned what he'd been doing and when she'd questioned him in the pub he'd simply changed the subject.

Why wouldn't he talk about it? Why had he let her carry on believing that he didn't take work seriously?

Her fingers tightened on the clipping. 'Can I keep this or does Letty want it back?'

Laura shook her head. 'She said we could have it. She's got another one. She worships him.'

'Yes, well, that's hardly surprising,' Joanna said softly, folding the piece of paper carefully and slipping it into the pocket of her blouse. 'If he helped her as much as she said, she probably owes him a great deal.'

Laura sighed dreamily and wrapped her arms around her waist. 'And he saved that child's life. He's got it all, hasn't he, Dr Weston? Looks, money, brain and guts—'

'Yes, yes, thank you, Laura,' Joanna said, noticing with a certain wry amusement that looks and money were at the top of Laura's list. She, on the other hand, was more attracted to the brains and the courage of the man. Either way, she didn't need to hear Laura listing Seb's attributes. She was achingly aware of what they were without needing to have them emblazoned in neon lights.

'I wonder why he's never married, Dr Weston?'

'I really have no idea, Laura, and I don't think it's any of our business,' Joanna said quickly, ending the conversation before it had begun. Even less did she need to have a conversation about Seb's private life with Laura.

'Women never stop ringing him,' Laura said innocently, unaware that her words were sending needles of pain through her employer's heart. 'At least twice a day he speaks to someone, usually someone different—often that Gabby woman.'

Gabby...

What exactly did Gabby mean to Seb?

Joanna made a supreme effort to pull herself together and bent to pick up her bag. 'I'll be in my room, Laura, if anyone wants me.'

'Right you are, Dr Weston,' Laura said cheerfully, bustling through to Reception to answer the phone that had just started to ring. 'I'll bring you a coffee later.'

Joanna closed the door of her room behind her and sat down at her desk, slowly pulling the crumpled newsclipping out of her pocket.

Dr Dare.

What risks had he taken to save that child? What hardship had he put himself through to work in such ferociously dangerous surroundings?

Suddenly all the barriers that she'd built between herself and Seb fell away, and she was left to face the painful truth.

He wasn't the frivolous, fun-seeking playboy that she'd dismissed him as being. He wasn't a work-shy joker who was afraid of commitment.

He was a dedicated doctor with a warm heart and the generosity to use his skills where they were needed most.

And she loved him.

Dear God, she loved him.

Which meant that she was in big trouble.

CHAPTER EIGHT

JOANNA had two emergency calls during her afternoon surgery and she was running so late that by the time she finished there was no sign of Seb.

'He said to tell you he'd be back later,' Laura said, locking one of the drawers behind the reception area. 'Is it all right if I go home now, Dr Weston?'

'Of course, Laura.' Joanna gave her a warm smile. 'And thank you for staying so late.'

'You're welcome.' Laura scooped up her bag and walked jauntily out of the surgery, leaving Joanna to lock the door behind her.

So Seb had gone out.

Why should that disappoint her? There was nothing between them after all. Only a couple of kisses, which wouldn't mean anything to a man like him.

The prospect of a lonely evening by herself in the house stretched dismally in front of her, and she gave a groan as she realised just how much having Seb around had changed her life.

Suddenly she didn't want to spend her evenings working. Or reading. Or even riding Romeo.

She wanted to be with Seb.

Which was utterly ridiculous, she chided herself firmly, because he quite clearly didn't feel the same way. For some strange, unfathomable reason he did seem to find her attractive, but that was probably just because he saw her as a challenge.

Just as Charlie had...

She bit her lip. But Seb wasn't like Charlie. She knew he wasn't.

On the other hand, she was older and wiser now and she should have more sense than to think even for a minute that a man like Seb could ever be seriously interested in a woman like her. If the idea weren't so sad it would be laughable.

Damn the man for making her feel this way…

Trying to distract herself, she phoned George Mills in Australia, ascertained that the baby was still making good progress but that her partner had no intention of coming home in the near future, then wandered through to the kitchen and made herself some scrambled eggs.

She'd just settled herself at the kitchen table to eat her lonely supper when she heard the sound of a key in the front door. Instantly her spirits lifted and she put down her fork, her smile of welcome fading as Seb entered the room, his handsome face drawn and tired.

'You look awful.' Joanna half stood, worried about the way he looked. 'Has something happened?'

He sank into a chair and ran a hand over his face with a groan. 'Not really. I just haven't had the best of days.'

Joanna slowly sat back down. 'I haven't had the best of days either, Seb,' she said quietly. 'Today I found out just how much of yourself you've been hiding from me.'

His eyes narrowed. 'If this is about Letty…'

'Not just Letty.' She reached into her pocket and pulled out the crumpled news clipping, dropping it onto the table between them.

He stared at it in silence, his dark jaw suddenly tense.

'Where did you get that?' His voice was hoarse and she swallowed, sensing that she was treading on private territory.

'Does it matter?'

'Yes.' Slowly he reached out and picked up the clipping,

an expression of distaste on his face as he stared down at it. With a rough exclamation he crumpled it in his fist and tossed it in the bin. 'I'd hoped I'd never see that clipping again.'

'Why?'

There was a long silence while he stared down at his hands and then he finally spoke. 'Because it reminds me of one of the worst times of my life. So many people died, buried under the rubble. It was a living nightmare. People digging with their bare hands, trying to get to loved ones…'

'But you saved that child.'

Seb gave a short laugh. 'Just one, Joanna. Just one. Barely noticeable in the big scheme of things.'

'I'm sure her parents noticed,' Joanna said softly, the words dying on her lips as she saw the bleak look in his eyes.

'Her parents were killed.'

'I'm sorry.' Joanna's voice was less than a whisper and he gave a tired smile.

'Don't be. She was luckier than some. Her grandparents are alive and an aunt. She isn't totally alone.'

Joanna couldn't even begin to imagine just how terrible it must have been. No wonder he didn't want to be re-minded of it all.

'In that picture, they called you an unknown doctor. Why didn't you tell them who you were?'

'Tell the press?' He shook his head. 'No, thanks. Once people know who I am, all they focus on is the money, my family background. My medical skills don't count any more. I didn't want that sort of publicity. Over there I was just a doctor doing a job like everyone else.'

Impulsively she reached across the table and took his hand. 'Why did you go?'

He gave a wry smile. 'They needed doctors.'

'It must have been terrible.'

He hesitated for a brief moment and then his fingers closed over hers and he started to talk, telling Joanna about the death and the fear and the relentless work, often for days and nights without sleep.

'You should have told me,' she said finally, unable to believe what she'd been hearing. It was so far removed from the civilised, protected environment that she worked in. 'You should have told me exactly what jobs you'd been doing. I can't believe the things I said to you, the things I believed about you.'

His grip tightened on her hand and his eyes locked with hers. 'It doesn't matter. We both made mistakes about each other, Joanna. I did the same thing about you.'

Their eyes held and she swallowed hard, soft colour touching her cheeks.

'Can I make you some supper or did you eat while you were out?'

'No, I didn't eat. And I'd love some supper.' He looked at her plate, giving a genuine smile for the first time that evening. 'Toast again? Haven't I taught you anything?'

'But this time with egg,' she pointed out hastily. 'Protein, Dr Macaulay. Protein. But I'll make you something different.'

'No need. Scrambled eggs are fine,' he murmured, releasing her hand and standing up in a fluid movement. 'What I really need is a hug.'

She tried to ignore the ridiculous reaction of her heart. 'A hug...'

'Yes, a hug.' He moved round the table and pulled her against him, his hands sliding over the soft fabric of her skirt and over the swell of her bottom. 'You feel good, Joanna. Really, really good.'

So did he. *Oh, so did he.*

She melted against the heat of his body, her eyes closed, loving the rough, clean, male smell that teased her nostrils.

'Seb?' She pulled away slightly and looked up at him.
'Can I ask you something?'

He gave a groan and gently stroked her blonde hair away
from her neck. 'Have you no sense of timing, woman? You
want to talk?'

'Yes.' Her voice was urgent. 'Today's been a shock for
me, Seb. You've hidden so much of yourself away that I
feel as though I don't know you…'

He slid his hands into her hair and tilted her face to his.
'You do know me, sweetheart.'

The soft endearment made Joanna's stomach turn over
and her heart stumble in her chest. 'But I don't. I kept
thinking— I thought that you—'

'You know me.' Seb's voice was firm. 'I'm the same
person, Joanna. The job I do doesn't change who I am.'

'Can I ask you a question?'

He smiled. 'Of course.'

'I wanted to ask you about Letty.' She nibbled her lip.
'What happened to her, Seb?'

'Letty?' He gave a sigh and sat down on the chair, pulling her onto his lap. 'She was eight years old when she had
her accident,' he said heavily. 'Some idiot had too many
drinks at lunchtime and then got behind the wheel. Letty
was walking to her ballet class.'

Joanna closed her eyes briefly as a clear image of the
accident floated in front of her brain.

'Her parents were so wrapped up in their own guilt and
grief that they didn't have anything left to give their little
girl.' Seb swallowed hard and his mouth was set in a grim
line. 'By the time I met her she'd virtually given up on
life. Everyone treated her as an invalid.'

Hesitantly, Joanna reached out and touched his hand.
'Except you.'

'That was part of what the charity was for,' he said
gruffly. 'To try and help the children make the best of what-

ever abilities they had. And to try and help the parents adapt. Having a disabled child is never easy.'

There was a long silence. 'I wish you'd told me.' Joanna's voice was soft. 'You knew what I thought when you told me that you'd been a doctor on a cruise ship. I thought that it was just another fun experience for you, pandering to the idle rich with indigestion and varicose veins. I never knew— I never guessed...'

He shrugged. 'It isn't something I talk about much. I do it on a fairly regular basis in one form or another but, to be honest, it's nice to escape from it some of the time. It was a very stressful winter in many ways. Letty wasn't the only one who was giving up on life. There were several others and, believe me, it's physically and emotionally draining, looking after those kids twenty-four hours a day.'

'I'm sure.' Joanna looked into his eyes. 'Seb, I'm sorry. For all the times I was rude about your attitude to work.'

'Don't be—you were partly right. I do like variety and I do like enjoying myself. Because I've seen enough to know that you ought to live life to the full every single day. But I'm not quite the selfish individual you imagined. Or at least I hope I'm not.'

'I know you're not.' She frowned slightly. 'I never do anything for charity.'

'But you do plenty for the people of this community.' He looked at her thoughtfully. 'But if you fancy doing something for charity then you could help me out at the weekend.'

'How?'

'There's a charity ball in London,' he told her, watching her reaction carefully. 'I've promised to go. Will you come as my partner?'

Her eyes widened and she stared at him in stunned silence. He wanted her to go to a ball?

'How would that help the charity?'

'Well, it wouldn't, but it would help me,' he admitted with boyish frankness. 'I don't really want to go, but if you were there…'

She licked dry lips. 'If I was there, what?'

His gaze flickered to her mouth and tension flared between them. 'Let's just say I'd enjoy an evening in your company.'

Their eyes met and suddenly Joanna could hardly breathe.

'I don't know Seb, I don't think—'

'Good idea,' he teased softly, placing a finger over her mouth to interrupt her objections. 'Don't think. Just say yes.'

Joanna looked at him doubtfully. 'I've never been to a ball before.'

'All the more reason to go,' he said softly, his finger tracing the line of her lower lip, his eyes devouring hers hungrily. 'Also, it will solve the problem of you being on your own in the house. I'm not prepared to leave you alone again but I promised them I'd go. So I find myself in a dilemma.'

'I haven't got anything to wear,' she said lamely, trying to ignore the sensations that his touch seemed to ignite in her body.

He shrugged carelessly. 'So we'll arrive in London early enough to find you something,' he murmured, his breathing slightly uneven as he watched her carefully. 'Say yes, Joanna.'

Yes?

To a weekend with this dangerous, stunningly handsome, sexy man who she knew she loved more than anything else in the world?

It was playing with fire…

'Where would we stay?'

'I'll sort that out.'

His touch was driving her wild.

'And what about the practice?'

'Ah, work!' His eyes teased her. 'Your favourite word. We'll arrange cover. Next?'

She felt herself drowning in the fathomless depths of his blue eyes. 'What do you mean, next?'

'What's your next excuse?' His expression was gentle. 'Come on, Joanna, you don't need to hunt for excuses. You can trust me. It's just a date and I'm not Charlie…'

A date?

But what exactly would the date entail? What did he want from her? What did he expect?

She felt so confused. She didn't know what he wanted. And she didn't know what she wanted either.

'I'm not the right sort of person for you to date,' she blurted out finally, her fingers trembling as they raked her blonde hair away from her eyes. 'I'm not smooth, I'm not an "it" girl—'

'It's you I want, Joanna,' he said softly, 'not an "it" girl. You.'

She shook her head, nerves mingling with excitement inside her. 'No. I'm not— I don't…'

She broke off and he lifted a dark eyebrow quizzically. 'You don't what?'

Joanna forced herself to look at Seb. 'I'm not that mad about sex,' she muttered finally, her eyes sliding away from his and hot colour filling her cheeks. 'I don't have anything to offer you. I'll disappoint you.'

There was a long silence and then he gave a sigh. 'Joanna, look at me.'

His voice was gruff and she stiffened slightly as he slipped his fingers under her chin and lifted her face to his.

'I don't think your experience with Charlie exactly counts, do you? And I can tell you that you won't disappoint me.'

'But—'

'You won't,' he said firmly, a faint smile playing around his firm mouth. 'And anyway, I'm not inviting you with an ulterior motive. This isn't a crafty plan to seduce you, Joanna. I'm not like that. I want you—very much—but only if you want me, too. We're not going to do anything you don't want to do. I'm inviting you to a ball to have fun. Eat, dance, chat. No strings attached. If, at the end of the evening, you want to say goodnight and go back to your room, that's fine by me.'

She loved his honesty but at the same time it made her even more confused. He wanted her. He'd spelt it out so that there could be no misunderstanding. Which meant that the decision was all hers...

Her heart was thudding so hard she could barely think straight.

'But—'

'Aha!' He grinned. 'Your second favourite word after "work". No buts, Joanna. Just say yes.'

She was silent for a moment and his smile faded as he searched her eyes.

'You can trust me, Joanna.'

Trust him?

Maybe she could trust him. It was herself she wasn't sure about. She wanted him so badly she ached inside, and it was such an alien feeling that she didn't know what she was going to do about it.

'Can I ask you something else?'

'Of course.'

'Why haven't you invited Gabby?'

His expression was suddenly guarded. 'Because I want to take you,' he said quietly. 'But only if you want to come. I'm not pushing you, Joanna.'

No. He wasn't the sort of man to put pressure on anyone.

He believed that everyone should make their own decisions in life.

What exactly did she mean to him?

He clearly liked her and found her attractive, but presumably he felt the same way about Gabby if the number of times he saw her was anything to go by.

No, if she went it had to be with her eyes open. He was inviting her as just another one of the women he liked to date and have fun with. So maybe she'd go and do just that. Have fun. And she'd worry about the rest later.

'All right,' she said finally, the beginnings of a smile playing around her full mouth. 'Thank you. I'd really like to come.'

'You would?' A sexy grin spread across his face. 'That's great. I'll make arrangements.'

All Joanna could think about for the rest of the week was the ball.

Part of her was apprehensive. But part of her was excited. *Very excited.*

She'd never actually been to a ball before, and suddenly she felt like a child.

And if she worried occasionally about what Seb would expect from her, well, she pushed the thought away, determined not to get herself in a stew. He'd said that she should treat it as a date, as a fun night out, and that's exactly what she intended to do.

With only a few days to go before her weekend away she worked hard in the surgery, making sure that everything was as up to date as possible before leaving the practice in the capable hands of the GPs from the neighbouring practice who had kindly volunteered to help out.

She received a message from the consultant in old-age psychiatry and when she called him back he confirmed that he'd visited Vera Peters and made an assessment.

Joanna was pleased and surprised that he'd managed to fit in a visit to see the old lady so quickly. 'What did you think?'

'Well, I confirm your provisional diagnosis of dementia,' the consultant told her, and Joanna gave a sigh.

'I was really hoping that we'd be able to keep them together at home. They've been married for forty years, you know.'

'Yes, her son gave me all the details.' The consultant paused, obviously reading his notes on the case. 'I think with the right social interventions we should be able to avoid admission. The husband is obviously keen to have her at home.'

'I didn't prescribe tranquillisers,' Joanna told him and he gave a murmur of approval.

'Quite right, too. In my experience they just increase confusion and the risk of falls.'

'What about hypnotics?'

'There's a growing feeling that they may irreversibly worsen dementia and confusion so I think it's best to steer clear of those as well if we can. If her behaviour becomes very disturbed, we could use a small amount of an atypical antipsychotic for just a short time. In my experience, difficult behaviour is usually transitory.'

'So you think that with the right support she should be able to manage at home?'

'Absolutely.' There was a pause. 'Social Services are going to contact some of the local voluntary groups so that should be a help for them.'

They talked for a while about the case and the involvement of the community mental health team, and by the time Joanna came off the phone she was feeling reassured that Vera was at least in good hands.

She sorted through a stack of results, noting which patients needed to be called back for further tests and treatment.

Her last patient of the morning was a fifty-year-old woman. Joanna knew her vaguely from previous consultations.

'What can I help you with, Mrs Swinton?'

The woman looked embarrassed and uncomfortable. 'I can hardly bear to tell you, to be honest. I've had this for two years so don't ask me why I'm coming to see you now, Doctor…'

'Had what, Mrs Swinton?' Joanna's tone was sympathetic. 'There's no need to be embarrassed. I'm a doctor— you can talk to me about anything.'

Mrs Swinton took a deep breath. 'I wet myself, doctor.' Her cheeks went scarlet. 'It's been happening for a while, as I said, but lately it's getting ridiculous. I never go out now unless I know in advance where all the toilets are in case I get caught short. I plan my whole life around where toilets are!'

Joanna listened carefully. 'How many times a day would you say that you need to use the toilet?'

Mrs Swinton gave a shrug. 'At least ten. Possibly more if I'm honest. And it's ruling my whole life. I don't go anywhere now unless I can drive myself. At least that way I can stop the car when I need to. I don't know why I'm telling you this—it's very embarrassing and I don't suppose for a moment that you'll be able to do anything about it.'

'We should certainly be able to do something about it,' Joanna contradicted her firmly. 'It sounds as though what you're suffering from is urge incontinence. Basically your bladder is working overtime!'

Mrs Swinton looked at her gloomily. 'So what can be done about that?'

Joanna reached for a pen and the appropriate form. 'First of all I want you to give me a specimen so that I can test it for signs of infection and also for glucose. Then I'm going to send you for something called urodynamic studies.'

'At the hospital?'

Joanna nodded. 'Yes, but only as an outpatient. After that, providing everything is fine—which I'm sure it will be—we'll do two things, Mrs Swinton. Firstly we're going to try and retrain your bladder.'

Mrs Swinton looked doubtful. 'How do we do that?'

'By gradually increasing the time between visits to the toilet,' Joanna told her. 'The second thing we'll do is to give you some drugs. There are drugs which work on the bladder to stop it being so active. They can be very effective.'

Mrs Swinton looked considerably more cheerful. 'So you don't think I need to resign myself to being like this for ever? I'm spending a fortune on pads and it's so embarrassing!!'

'We'll do our best to sort it out,' Joanna assured her, explaining in more detail about the tests she wanted to perform.

By the time she finished her surgery it was late and she was exhausted. She walked through to the house, locked the connecting door and made her way to the kitchen.

Seb was busy cooking and she sank onto one of the kitchen chairs with a groan.

'I'm not sure I'm going to make it this weekend after all.'

He turned with a frown on his face. 'Joanna—'

'Just kidding.' She smiled weakly. 'It's just that I'm exhausted. I can barely walk, let alone dance.'

He smiled and turned back to the supper. 'You'll be fine. Nice dinner. Hot bath. Early to bed.'

Just the mention of bed was enough to make her blush,

and she looked away quickly so that she didn't have to focus on those broad shoulders.

They ate supper, chatting about their day and the patients they'd seen.

'So, is everything in place for the weekend?' Seb pushed the salad towards her and she nodded.

'Yes. I've arranged all the cover.'

'Good.' Seb took a mouthful of wine. 'And have you told Laura?'

Joanna hesitated. 'No. Not yet.'

'It's the day after tomorrow, Joanna,' Seb pointed out gently. 'Don't you think it's time you told her that you're going away?'

Joanna bit her lip. 'There'll be gossip, Seb. You know what this place is like.'

'Probably.' His voice was soft and his eyes were sympathetic. 'And does that bother you?'

'I'm not sure.'

Did it bother her? Did she really care what people thought of her? For once in her life she was throwing caution to the wind and behaving in a way she'd never behaved before.

'I've had an idea.' Seb gave her a wicked grin and she looked at him suspiciously.

'What?'

'Why don't we put a notice in the newsagent window? I'm sure that Doris Parker would be only too happy to oblige, and it would mean that they'd hear the right story.'

Joanna laughed but her insides churned uncomfortably. The right story? She wasn't sure that she knew what the right story was. What exactly did Seb think of her? And what were his plans? She knew that he wasn't playing with her like Charlie had, but he hadn't said anything to imply that he was serious either. Was she just a convenient amusement for him while he was in Devon?

Or did she mean something more to him?

CHAPTER NINE

JOANNA managed to keep her proposed trip a secret from Laura until Friday but it was inevitable that the girl would find out eventually.

'*He's taking you to a ball?*' Laura gave a sigh, glassy-eyed with envy. 'Just like Cinderella…'

'I hope not, Laura,' Seb drawled, strolling into Reception and dropping a pile of results onto the desk. 'If she turns into a pumpkin at midnight, I'll be seriously embarrassed.'

Joanna forced a smile, trying to disguise how anxious she was about the whole thing. As far as she was concerned, she might well be turning into a pumpkin at midnight. There was the dress, for one thing—she wasn't used to buying ballgowns with only a few hours to spare. Seb had assured her that they'd arrive in London in time to find her something perfect, but how could he be so confident? Was he that experienced at tracking down suitable women's clothing at short notice?

Maybe he was, she thought miserably, slinking out of Reception and walking back to her consulting room. He certainly had enough women chasing after him. Gabby had called again during the week, along with a Katrin and a Helena. Which all just proved that he wasn't short of female company.

So what on earth was he doing with her? Was she just novelty value again? The studious vicar's daughter?

She threw herself into her surgery, seeing the usual stream of minor ailments, interspersed with the odd worrying case. She arranged an urgent referral for one young woman with a breast lump who had a family history of breast cancer and referred a severe case of psoriasis to a dermatologist.

Young Freddie Dover came back to see her and Joanna was delighted by the improvement in his skin.

'I can see you haven't been scratching anywhere near as much.' She praised him warmly and the little boy grinned.

'I've been patting. Not scratching.'

'Good for you,' Joanna said, smiling at his mother. 'Keep up the emollients, Mrs Dover. He needs to have plenty of grease on his skin to keep it moist.'

Mrs Dover nodded. 'We're getting through masses of stuff but it does seem to be working, doesn't it?'

They left the room and Joanna quickly wrote up the notes and then called her next patient.

At the end of her surgery Seb came in to discuss a couple of his cases, and they explored the pros and cons of various treatments.

'By the way,' he said as he stood up to leave, 'I forgot to ask you what happened with Vera Peters. You saw the whole family at the beginning of the week, didn't you?'

'Oh.' She sighed as she thought about Vera. 'It's not looking that great. I checked her vascular risk factors, checked her for infections, anaemia, other organic conditions. I ran a whole raft of blood tests and did the abbreviated mental test score, but it looks as though it is dementia. The consultant has visited and assessed her, and he agreed.'

Seb frowned. 'Are they capable of managing on their own at the moment, do you think?'

'I think so.' Joanna nodded slowly. 'The problem is assessing the risk to poor John. Vera is so emotionally labile and her memory is so poor that she isn't the easiest person to live with, but I'm hoping that we can have a mixture of day care and help in the home so that we can keep them together. They've been married for forty years.'

Her eyes misted and Seb rolled his eyes and smiled.

'You're a marshmallow, Joanna Weston.'

'Possibly.' She cleared her throat and took a deep breath. 'Listen, about tomorrow—'

'If you're thinking of changing your mind, I'm definitely not listening,' he warned, standing up in a smooth movement and making for the door of her consulting room.

Joanna felt her heart tumble in her chest at the thought of the weekend.

What was going to happen?

'I wasn't changing my mind,' she said quickly, cursing inwardly as she felt herself blush. 'I was just going to say that I've arranged for cover from midmorning, so I'll do Saturday surgery and then we can leave.'

The thought of spending a weekend with Seb did strange things to her insides.

'Which should get us there in time to find you a dress, settle into the hotel and get ready for the evening,' he agreed. 'Excellent.'

Was it?

She was beginning to wonder.

The hotel foyer was sumptuous. Cool marble floors, crystal chandeliers and elegant sofas.

And everyone knew Seb.

'Good to see you again, Dr Macaulay. We have your usual suite.' The man reached for a key, handed it over and called for a porter to deal with their luggage with a discreet snap of his fingers.

His usual suite?

Joanna stood to one side, desperately self-conscious in her simple cotton skirt and top. Suddenly she felt as gauche and out of place as she always had as a child. She was the vicar's daughter again.

'You look gorgeous,' Seb whispered in her ear as they

walked towards the lift. 'And incredibly sexy. Straight out of a bad boy's dreams. Have I told you lately that I want you badly?'

Warmed by his words, her eyes flickered to his and the look in them brought faint colour to her cheeks.

'And you're the only woman I know who still knows how to blush,' he murmured, giving her a sexy wink and pressing the button for the top floor.

It wasn't until he opened the door of the room that her mind suddenly clicked into action.

'Are we sharing a room? You said I'd have my own room.'

Seb ushered her through the door and closed it behind them. 'It's a suite, Joanna,' he reassured her gently. 'Two bedrooms, bathroom, living room, balcony. Plenty of room for you to have space and privacy.' He paused, his eyes searching hers. 'If that's what you want…'

Joanna's eyes slid away from his and she felt her heart rate pick up speed. What exactly did she want? She didn't know.

'What's that?' She frowned, her attention caught by a pile of expensive bags next to the window.

'Our shopping.' For once in his life Seb suddenly looked unsure of himself. 'I thought you might be too tired to go out so I rang a few places and asked them to send a selection of things over, but if there's nothing you like we can always start again.'

Shops had *sent things over*? And not just any old shops if the elegant bags were anything to go by. But, then, that was the sort of service that the Macaulay name attracted—or the Macaulay millions…

'They're for me?' She stared at the bags and then back at him, astonishment in her eyes. 'But how did you know my size?'

He gave a boyish shrug. 'I guessed. Probably all wrong—why don't you take a look?'

Warily Joanna walked towards the bags and opened them one by one, laying the contents over the sofa.

'Do you like them?' For once Seb's legendary confidence seemed to be under threat, and Joanna smiled.

'They're beautiful,' she said softly, fingering the silky fabric of the first dress with reverent fingers. 'Can I try them on?'

He let out a long breath, his relief evident. 'Of course. Why don't you use the bedroom? Give me a shout if you need any help.'

She didn't. There were three dresses, all more elegant than anything she'd ever owned, or even dreamed of, before. She should have been spoilt for choice, but she wasn't because she knew instantly which one she was going to wear.

The red one.

It was glamorous and sexy and transformed her instantly into the sort of woman that she'd often dreamed of being when she'd been younger.

Maybe Seb was right, she thought, staring in disbelief at the miraculous transformation in the mirror. Maybe she *was* pretty. She certainly *felt* pretty.

There was a tap on the door and she quickly slid out of the dress and back into her practical cotton skirt.

'Just coming…'

Joanna hung the dress on the hanger, touched it softly one last time and then placed it in the wardrobe along with the others.

Seb was waiting on the other side of the doorway, one eyebrow lifted expectantly.

'No good?'

'Perfect.' Her eyes shone with excitement at the prospect of wearing the dress, and he grinned.

'But you're not showing me?'

'No way, Dr Macaulay.' She shook her head vigorously. 'No previews. You can wait until tonight.'

His smile faded and his eyes dropped to her mouth. 'Actually,' he said softly, 'I'm not sure that I can.'

The atmosphere between them was suddenly electric and her hand was shaking as she closed the bedroom door.

'Why don't you show me round this suite?' she suggested weakly, trying to break the powerful connection between them. 'It's so big I might get lost.'

'Coward.' With a wry smile he brushed her cheek with his knuckles and held out his hand. 'Come on, then—let's have the grand tour.'

She took a deep breath as Seb's warm, strong fingers closed over hers and then followed him across the soft carpet to the bathroom.

He opened the door and she gasped in astonishment. It was the height of luxury, dominated by a large corner spa bath, surrounded by glistening white marble and exotic plants.

'Seb, it's bigger than the living room,' she murmured, secretly longing to slip into the deep tub. What luxury! She'd only ever seen a bathroom like that in the movies!

'Come and see the rest.' He led her out of the bathroom, onto the balcony with its view across Hyde Park and the rooftops of London.

She looked at him in stunned amazement. 'Do you always live like this?'

He smiled down at her. 'You know I don't. At the moment I'm living with you. Before that I spent six months on a ship, sharing cramped quarters with twenty extremely traumatised children, and before that I was working in the blazing heat under a ton of rubble. Hardly luxury.'

'You do all that,' she muttered, still humbled by the selfless work that he'd done, 'and you don't actually have to work at all.'

'Ah, but it helps me score points with women,' he teased, slipping an arm around her shoulders and pulling her towards him. 'Seriously, though, work doesn't always have to be financially driven, Joanna. I work because it gives me satisfaction, and I'm luckier than most because my private income allows me to do the work I want to, irrespective of remuneration. I suspect that there are plenty of doctors who would love to do what I do, but they have families to support so it isn't an option.'

Joanna slipped off her shoes and curled up on the deep, comfortable sofa with a sigh of satisfaction.

'Well I still think you're amazing. And this is amazing. I think I could get used to this.' She smiled at him and he smiled back, settling himself in the chair opposite.

They talked all afternoon. Talked and laughed. He told her about things that had happened on the cruise and at fundraising events, how pompous people could be. She told him more about her childhood, opening up more than she ever had before in her life.

Eventually he glanced at his watch. 'I'm going to go for a quick swim in the pool before I get ready. If that's all right with you?'

'Of course.' She nodded immediately, thinking that it would give her time to get ready in peace and quiet.

The more she thought about it, the more she wanted to look her absolute best.

She wanted to surprise him.

Joanna stared at herself in the mirror, unable to believe that the sleek blonde staring back at her was really the same person who had arrived in London only a few hours earlier.

The hotel hairdresser, recruited at the last minute to turn Joanna's untamed curls into something more restrained, had worked wonders and her usually unmanageable bob was now a sleek blonde curtain hanging to her shoulders.

And the dress…

The dress was a red, silky dream, clinging to every curve of her body as if it had been painted on by a skilled artist with a wicked mind.

'Joanna? Are you ready?'

The sound of Seb's deep voice sent her pulse racing and she took a steadying breath, took a last look in the mirror and stepped out of the bedroom, pausing shyly in the doorway as she waited for his reaction.

'My God…' His voice was hoarse and he cleared his throat and stepped closer to her, his strong hands sliding up her bare arms and smoothing the blonde curtain of hair away from her shoulders. 'You look…stunning.'

With a self-conscious smile she glanced up at him, her eyes widening as she saw him in his dinner jacket, the cut accentuating the width of his shoulders and his powerful physique.

He was heart-stoppingly handsome and she felt her heart race away again, totally out of control.

'Perhaps we should just forget the ball,' he suggested, and she smiled up at him, her eyes shining.

'No way. You invited me on a date, Dr Macaulay, and you're not backing out now. I'm all dressed up and ready to party.'

Party…

Something she hadn't done for a long time. Maybe never. Certainly never like this.

Seb laughed out loud. 'I love you like this. Like a child with a new toy. Come on, then, Cinderella.' He held out his hand, his sexy eyes smiling down at her. 'Your carriage awaits.'

The ballroom was crowded with people and immediately the confidence oozed out of Joanna like air from a popped balloon. They were so beautiful, so stylish—and they all knew Seb.

He frowned down at her and his fingers tightened on hers as he sensed the change in her. 'What's the matter?'

She bit her lip. 'I don't fit…'

He muttered something under his breath and turned her to face him. 'Look at me,' he ordered softly. 'Look at me, Joanna.'

She did as she was told, her stomach lurching at the warmth and gentleness in his eyes.

'You do fit, Joanna. You're beautiful and elegant and you'd fit in anywhere.' He stroked a strand of blonde hair away from her face. 'Your problem is that you don't feel it inside. And we need to do something about that.'

His gaze burned into hers and for a moment he looked as though he wanted to say something more, but he wasn't given a chance. Someone caught his arm, wanting to greet him, shake his hand, catch up on gossip, and so it continued until they sat down for dinner.

Whichever way they turned he was stopped by someone, kissed by women, fawned over until Joanna was ready to scream. Several times she tried to melt into the background, sure that he didn't need or want her hanging onto his arm, but each time his grip on her hand tightened and he clamped her firmly to his side.

'Why are you trying to run off?' His tone was calmly amused as he watched her attempts to vanish into the crowd.

'I'm cramping your style,' she muttered, but he just gave her a lazy smile that made her knees weak.

'You are my style, sweetheart.' His eyes were full of promise and she felt her face heat.

He didn't mean it. He couldn't possibly mean it. Not with all these gorgeous beauties watching him from across the dance floor. And who could blame them? He was easily the most attractive man in the room. And probably one of the richest.

She stopped dead and stared at his handsome profile in dismay, realising just how impossible it all was. She'd fallen in love with a man who was worlds apart from her.

Oh, dear heaven, how had that happened? *When* had that happened? Somewhere between that first kiss and finding out just what a warm and generous human being he was. She'd wanted to hate him, wanted to hate his values, but his values had turned out to be sounder than hers.

As the waiters brought their food she stared at her plate in dismay, wondering whether she'd ever want to eat again.

She'd never actually thought that she could fall in love. Hadn't thought that she could feel that depth of emotion for a man.

But she had. And he was going to break her heart, she knew he was. What would a man like him want with a woman like her? Just temporary amusement? Nothing more, that was for sure.

'What's wrong?' Seb's soft tone was full of concern and she gave him a wide smile, determined not to give away her feelings. They were nothing to do with him, and they certainly weren't his fault.

He hadn't asked her to fall in love with him. All she had to do was eat dinner, go back to the room and then sleep safely in her own part of the suite until they could get back home.

But she'd forgotten about the dancing.

The minute the band started playing, Seb closed strong fingers around Joanna's wrist and led her firmly onto the dance floor, whirling her into a fast number that left her breathless and laughing. They danced and danced until the music slowed and finally he pulled her against him, the heat from his hard, muscular body burning through the delicate fabric of her dress.

She shivered with reaction as she felt his warm hand slide down her bare back, pulling her closer against him.

Suddenly breathing was difficult and she tried to concentrate on the music as they swayed on the dance floor, the tension between them steadily mounting.

Feeling the hard ridge of his erection pressing against her, she pulled away from him slightly, her face hot. 'Shouldn't you dance with someone else?'

'What? In this state?' He gave a low chuckle. 'I'll be arrested if you move now.'

'But people will talk.' She tried to pull away completely but she was clamped firmly against him.

'Let them talk,' he said hoarsely, moulding her body to his. 'The only person I want to dance with tonight is you.'

Trapped against him, she dragged the breath into her lungs, suddenly aware of every inch of his incredible physique.

'Joanna.' His voice was a groan, and she lifted her head to meet his tortured gaze. 'Are you ready to go back to our room?'

She stilled in his arms, her heart thudding, knowing exactly what he was asking.

What she didn't know was what her answer was going to be. Seb might want her but he didn't love her...

'Joanna?' His voice was urgent and her heart rate trebled.

'I'm ready.' Her voice was barely audible above the loud beat of the music, but she could see from the sudden darkening of his eyes that he'd heard her.

He kept a tight hold on her hand as the lift purred up to the top of the hotel, and then suddenly they were inside the subtly lit suite and she was shivering with anticipation.

Seb shouldered the door closed, locked it carefully and then lifted a hand and slowly removed his bow-tie.

His eyes never left hers, his gaze simmering with heat and intent as he unbuttoned the first few buttons of his shirt.

'Come here.' His soft command increased her nerves and she stared at his outstretched hand, her heart thudding in her chest.

He was leaving the decision to her. She could step forward or she could wish him goodnight.

'Seb…'

His eyes were suddenly incredibly gentle. 'There's nothing to be scared of, sweetheart.'

The endearment made her insides melt. 'I…' She swallowed painfully, 'What if it doesn't work?'

He gave her a grin that was arrogantly male. 'Oh, it'll work, Joanna. Trust me on that one.'

And she did trust him.

Just like Laura, she had little doubt that Seb would be good in bed. Experienced. Patient. Not fumbling and clumsy like Charlie.

So why was she hesitating?

She lifted her gaze to his, saw the healthy desire burning in his blue eyes and her hesitation melted away.

Without speaking she stepped forward, hoping that he'd make the next move. She didn't know what to do. She'd never seduced a man in her life before.

'Are you sure?' His voice was firm and his eyes searched hers thoroughly. 'I can sleep in the spare room…'

No. She didn't want that.

She shook her head, feeling incredibly shy as she saw passion flare in the depths of his gaze.

Without waiting for her to speak, he scooped her up in his arms and carried her through to the master bedroom, gently kicking the door shut behind them.

He lowered her to her feet as if she were made of glass, his hands sliding up her bare arms to rest on her shoulders.

'You are so beautiful.'

He bent his head and touched his lips to hers, kissing her slowly, kindling the fire that had been on a slow burn all evening.

His tongue gently traced the line of her lips and then dipped gently inside, exploring and tasting, deepening the kiss until the heat flared through her body.

Tentatively her tongue tangled with his, following his lead, and she felt a thrill of joy as he shuddered and drew her closer. His hand slid slowly down her back, taking the zip of her dress with it, and the red silk fabric whispered over her skin and floated down to the floor.

'You just lost your dress, Cinderella.' His deep voice was husky and for a moment she felt a stab of shyness as reality hit her.

What was she doing here? What was she doing in this man's arms?

She leaned her forehead against his broad chest, suddenly totally out of her depth. Overwhelmed by the feelings he aroused in her.

Hideously conscious of the fact that she was nearly naked and he was still fully dressed, she protested as he gently put her away from him.

'I want to look at you…' His gaze slid down her body and his breath caught. 'Oh, Joanna…'

The look in his eyes banished her shyness and she gave him a soft smile and lifted a hand to his shirt. 'Aren't you rather overdressed?'

Seb's breathing was unsteady. 'I didn't want to scare you by rushing things.'

Her heart pounded as he dealt with the buttons on his shirt, gradually exposing his chest. Her eyes followed the line of dark hair that led over his taut, muscular abdomen down into his trousers, and her mouth dried.

'Why don't you help me?' His soft suggestion made her shiver and she lifted a hand to the fastening of his trousers, hearing the breath hiss through his teeth as her flesh connected with his.

With shaking fingers she undid his trousers and slid the zip down, aware of the throbbing heat of his erection teasing the tips of her fingers.

With a rough exclamation he dispensed with the rest of his clothes, tossing them carelessly onto the floor, his eyes never leaving hers.

'You're shaking.' He cupped her cheek in his palm and she gave him a weak smile.

'Nerves…excitement… I don't know, Seb…'

His expression was suddenly serious. 'You know you can call a halt whenever you want?'

She hesitated and then shook her head. 'I don't want to.' She licked her lips. 'I want you.'

He lifted her in his arms and gently laid her on the bed, his breathing ragged as he lowered himself down beside her.

Her cheeks burned as she saw his gaze shift from her face and slide down her body. And then he bent his head and took one dusky pink nipple between his firm lips, drawing a gasp from her as he flicked it skillfully with his tongue before drawing it deep into the erotic warmth of his mouth.

Heat spread throughout her whole body and she shifted under him, arching towards him, unconsciously begging for more. Instantly he responded, turning his attention to her other breast, his mouth working the same magic until she was drowning in sensation, only dimly aware that his clever fingers were now resting lightly on the scrap of silk between her legs.

She was breathing as hard as if she'd run a marathon and her body wouldn't stay still. She wanted to move—she had to move—*move with him.*

He kissed his way back up her body to her mouth, his hand still resting teasingly on the silk of her panties.

'Seb...please...' She had no idea what she was begging him to do, but he must have known because even as he bent his head and started to kiss her, she felt his long fingers slip inside the flimsy silk and touch her for the first time.

She gave a shudder and clutched the hard muscle of his shoulders, writhing under his skilled touch. He seemed to know exactly how to touch her—where to touch her—and she couldn't stay still, her whole body twisting under his as he drove her to a frenzy.

Desperate for more of him, she reached down to touch him, too, but he caught her hand and shook his head.

'No, Joanna,' he muttered against her mouth as he licked at her full lips. 'I don't think my control is up to it. I want you so badly.'

She gave a sob and arched towards him. 'So why are you taking so long? Why don't you—'

'Because I want you to be ready,' he said softly, his fingers exploring her so intimately that she could barely concentrate on what he was saying.

'I am ready, Seb,' she gasped, feeling his muscles flex as he briefly lifted his weight off her and reached into the pocket of his trousers for a small foil packet.

Then he moved over her and took her mouth briefly in a sizzling kiss, his eyes locking with hers.

'Look at me, Joanna. I want you with me...'

Her breathing rapid, she felt him enter her slowly, his eyes holding hers as he pushed deeper, stretching and filling her with his pulsing strength.

'Oh, Seb.' She gave a sob and wrapped her legs around him, drawing him deeper, gasping as he thrust into the heart of her, joining them completely.

He paused, his breathing rapid, his body dominating and filling hers. 'I love you, Joanna.'

His words filled her heart and tears pricked her eyes.
Never before.

Not even in her dreams had she felt like this…

'I love you, too—with all my heart.'

And then he moved, slowly at first, shifting the angle so that he brushed against her sensitive breasts, so that he drew the maximum response from her quivering body. Gradually he increased the pace, driving her forward towards ecstasy then slowing down at the last moment, leaving her frantic for completion.

'Seb…please…'

He grinned down at her, a sheen of sweat on his handsome face. 'I'm torturing us both.'

And he was, his rigid control evident as he drove them both to the point of desperation.

He pushed her hair away from her face with an unsteady hand, his movements slow and deliberate as he moved inside her, his eyes never releasing hers.

'I love you, Joanna—remember that.' And then he built the rhythm again and instinctively Joanna knew that this was it. That this time he'd stopped the teasing.

And her body didn't feel like hers any more. She didn't recognise any of the feelings that were swelling inside her, spreading through her body like a tidal wave.

She cried out softly, her hands moving over the slick muscles of Seb's back as she held onto him, wanting to go wherever he intended to take her. And he took her all the way, his body demanding and controlling until she felt her body tighten and convulse, until she heard his harsh groan and felt the powerful thrusts of his completion.

And she held him tightly, heart racing, tears falling, knowing that what she felt for this man would stay with her for ever.

CHAPTER TEN

IT WAS the noise of the shower that woke Joanna.

She lay for a moment, disorientated and drowsy, and then gave a yawn and slid out of the huge bed. For a wild moment she was tempted to join Seb but remembering the intimacies they'd shared the night before, she felt impossibly shy. Instead, she wandered through to the living area of the suite and decided to wait for him there.

A fresh pot of coffee had been set on the table and she poured herself a cup and then flopped onto one of the comfy sofas.

And then she saw the picture.

She reached out and picked up the newspaper on the top of the pile, the coffee-cup clattering in the saucer as she put it back onto the table with a shaking hand.

The picture was of her.

Of her.

Well, her and Seb, to be precise—locked in a clinch that left the reader in no doubt that they were more than friends.

A sick feeling built in her stomach as she picked up another paper, heat flooding her face as she looked at the suggestive photo and read the caption MILLIONAIRE DOCTOR'S LATEST CONQUEST.

Was that how they all saw her? As just another one of his conquests?

Without even picking it up, she could see that a third paper had printed a similar picture but from a different angle so that the love shining out of her eyes was there for everyone to see.

Including Seb, presumably.

Judging from the way the papers were lying open, he'd obviously already seen them.

Suddenly Joanna felt chilled to the bone and she hugged the dressing-gown around her as if it could somehow give protection against prying eyes. *How could they do that?* How could they publish something so private? So personal?

It had been between her and Seb.

Or so she'd thought. Only just like her other, ill-fated relationship, it had soon become public property.

'Why does it always happen to me?' She stared at the pile of newspapers with dull eyes. 'Why, when I get involved with a man, does the whole world get to know every detail?'

Suddenly she was swamped by feelings that she'd suppressed for years. Once again she was an object of public interest, and she hated it.

What would happen now? She'd have to go back to her quiet little Devon village and face being the subject of gossip. And what gossip there would be. Her patients would probably take a little while to recognise the starry-eyed, wanton blonde in the photo as their own, staid Dr Weston, but when they did, well, they'd be talking for months to come.

She gave a groan and sank back onto the sofa, feeling physically sick.

And then the phone rang.

Wondering who could possibly be calling her, she got slowly to her feet and walked towards the bedroom, stopping dead as she saw Seb pick up the phone, his back to her.

A towel was wrapped loosely round his hips and his broad, muscular shoulders glistened with droplets of water from the shower. Her mouth dried and she remembered again the way his body had felt against hers.

Incredible…

She took a deep breath and forced herself to be rational. Seb wasn't responsible for what the newspapers printed, she reasoned. She'd been with him the whole time so she knew that he hadn't invited their attentions. She knew as well as the next person that you couldn't believe everything you read in the papers. So did he really see her as another conquest?

No.

She couldn't believe that. *She wouldn't.*

The sound of his deep voice as he answered the phone made her knees weak.

He had a gorgeous voice—deep and very, very sexy.

'Gabby, hi.' There was no missing the affection in his voice, and Joanna felt her stomach lurch.

Gabby?

What was she doing, calling their hotel room? How did she even know where they were? Couldn't the woman leave him alone even for one night?

Seb listened for a moment and then gave a short, bitter laugh. 'Yes, of course I saw the papers.'

Joanna closed her eyes. She shouldn't be eavesdropping. She should move away and leave him to talk in the privacy that he thought he had, but her feet were frozen to the floor. She couldn't have moved away if her life had depended on it.

'Stop worrying, Gab.' Seb's tone was gentle and reassuring. 'They're just a few photographs. They don't mean anything. My relationship with Joanna doesn't affect you and me at all. We carry on as normal, angel—you can relax.'

Carry on as normal?

Joanna felt the blood drain out of her face and she backed out of the bedroom and took refuge on the balcony, staring down at the cars below through a blur of tears. Had last night really meant so little to him that he intended to carry on seeing other woman?

No!

Her heart thudded painfully. He'd said that he loved her.

And she'd believed him.

Oh, dear God, she'd been stupid enough to believe him. But here he was telling Gabby that nothing was going to change between them.

She might have been wrong about his commitment to his work, but she'd obviously been right in her assessment of him as a playboy. Seb just wasn't the right sort of man for her. She wanted a man who was going to love her and her alone. She would never be able to accept him seeing other women.

What was she going to do?

Feeling sick inside, she forced herself to face the unpleasant truth. Seb didn't love her. Not the way she wanted him to love her. Which meant that the only thing she could do was lift her chin high and leave fast, before he came to find her.

Going back inside, she glanced into the bedroom. It was empty, which presumably meant that Seb was back in the bathroom.

Making as little noise as possible, she dragged on her clothes, stuffed her few belongings into her bag and gave a final, painful glance at the red dress which lay in a pool on the carpet, a poignant reminder of their one night of passion.

With a last glance towards the bathroom she took a deep breath and walked quietly across the thick carpet towards the door, letting herself out quietly and making her way downstairs.

Somehow she'd make her own way home. He'd follow her, of course. He had to. After all, he was still living with

her. But at least she didn't have to face him until she'd
worked out what to do.

The taxi drove through the village and Joanna felt hideously self-conscious as she saw people that she knew well
wandering about their daily business.

Had they all read the papers?

Were they all talking about her?

She paid the taxi driver and stepped out onto the gravel
drive outside the house.

'Oh, Dr Weston.' Alice James immediately scurried over,
her face pink with excitement. 'I was on my way to church
but I was hoping I'd catch you because I wanted to say
how thrilled we all are. We were all hoping for it, of
course.'

Joanna stared at her. 'Thrilled about what, Alice? Hoping
for what?'

'You and Dr Macaulay getting together.' Alice beamed
at her. 'We always knew you were a good match. Ever
since that day you had lunch in the pub together we've all
been crossing our fingers.'

'Lunch in the—' Joanna broke off, appalled by what she
was hearing. 'But it wasn't a date, Alice. It was just lunch,
for goodness' sake. And anyway, how did you know?'

They'd been miles from the village. Miles! Surely there
hadn't been anyone around that knew her?

'Well, Doris Parker's niece works in the pub, and she
recognised Dr Macaulay's car,' Alice told her cheerfully,
and Joanna closed her eyes and gave a sigh.

Of course—the car. It was hardly the most discreet mode
of transport. And if Doris Parker knew then she might as
well have advertised the fact in neon lights that she and
Seb had eaten lunch together.

'It was just lunch,' Joanna repeated firmly, but Alice
gave her a knowing smile and patted her hand.

'Lunch, followed by a trip up to the coast and a romantic walk…'

Joanna's eyes widened. 'Alice are you following me? How did you?' she stopped, shaking her head with a groan. 'No, you don't even tell me how you knew. I suppose Doris has another niece who lives by the coast?'

'Nothing to do with Doris,' Alice said happily. 'Tom Kenton had gone over that way to take a look at some sheep, and he happened to notice you both.'

'Well, it's great to know that I'll never get lost anywhere,' Joanna said weakly, fumbling in her bag for her keys. 'There'll always be someone who knows who I am and where I come from.'

'That's because you're our doctor and you're important to us,' Alice said firmly. 'Anyway, we couldn't have been more thrilled when we saw it all in the papers this morning.'

Joanna dropped the keys and closed her eyes. So that was what this was all about. The picture in the papers. She might have known that nothing would slip past Alice.

'You can't believe everything you read in the papers,' she mumbled, stopping to retrieve the keys. 'I helped Dr Macaulay out by going to the ball with him. It didn't mean anything. The papers got it all wrong.'

'Oh no!' Alice frowned and shook her head vigorously. 'I saw the way you were looking at him. *And the way he was looking at you.* Papers may lie, dear, but cameras never do.'

Oh, yes, they did. Everything that had happened with Seb had been a lie.

She swallowed down the lump in her throat and opened the front door. 'It's just your imagination, Alice,' Joanna said heavily as she stepped inside the house. 'There's nothing going on between Dr Macaulay and me. Nothing at all.

Now, if you'll excuse me, I've got to dash and turn off the alarm before the whole of the police force comes visiting.'

Alice gave a puzzled frown, suddenly looking distracted. 'Of course, dear. We'll see you later. But I'm sure you—'

'Thank you, Alice,' Joanna said gently, sliding inside and closing the door firmly behind her.

What a nightmare. She could just imagine what was happening in the village. The whole community was obviously discussing her romance with Seb.

With a groan she switched off the alarm, made herself a cup of tea and then changed into her jodphurs. She'd go for a ride. At least on the back of a horse she could usually escape the locals!

Joanna had been riding for two hours when she heard the steady thud of hooves in the distance and saw a horse and rider approaching.

It was Seb. On a horse that she didn't recognise.

For a wild moment she contemplated riding off in the other direction, but immediately rejected the idea. What was the point? He'd only come after her and, anyway, she'd have to face him some time.

So she stood her ground, waiting until he drew close.

'I didn't know you rode.' She could see at a glance that he rode well, with the easy confidence of someone who was perfectly at home in the saddle.

'There's a lot of things you don't know about me, Joanna, remember?' His gaze was steady on hers.

'What are you doing here, Seb?' She looked away, terrified that she'd throw herself at him and make a fool of herself. How could she ever have thought that a man like him would be interested in a woman like her? She must have been delusional.

He raised an eyebrow. 'I can't believe you're seriously asking me that question. You owe me an explanation,

Joanna. And don't even try and pretend that you don't know what I'm talking about.'

She shifted slightly in the saddle, fighting back tears. 'It wouldn't have worked, Seb. This thing between us.' The tears seemed to be sitting in her throat. 'I was stupid to think it could.'

'It worked well enough last night,' he said pointedly, and she closed her eyes, refusing to allow herself to remember just how amazing their night together had been.

'Seb—'

'Come on, Joanna.' His voice was rough and he urged his horse closer to hers so that they were side by side. 'Something spooked you and I have a right to know what it was. Was it the photographs? I know you saw them and I was kicking myself for not hiding them before I'd had a chance to warn you. I know what a private person you are,' Seb said carefully, and she glared at him through unshed tears.

'So why didn't you stop them taking those photos?'

He swore under his breath and closed his eyes briefly. 'Because I wasn't thinking about photographers. I was just thinking about you. Us. And do you know why the press were interested last night? Because for once they saw me smitten with a woman.'

Joanna felt intensely vulnerable. When he spoke like that it was so easy to believe him. So tempting. 'They said I was another one of your conquests.'

'Well, they were wrong,' Seb said softly. 'And if you really want me to, I'll ring them and tell them, although I don't see why we should help sell their newspapers.'

'It wasn't just the photos,' she burst out, hurt that he didn't understand the reason she'd left. 'I can't share you Seb. I thought it didn't matter but it does. *It does.*'

'*Share me?*' He looked genuinely amazed. 'What the hell

do you mean, share me? Who do you think you're sharing me with?'

She looked at him, knowing that the depth of her agony was reflected in her eyes. 'I can't be one of several women in your life. I just can't.'

'One of several—' He shook his head as if to clear it. 'I don't know what you're talking about, Joanna. Are you saying that you think I'm involved with someone else?'

Her eyes slid away from his.

'Joanna, look at me!!' He made an impatient sound and ducked his head so that he could see her face. 'After everything we shared last night, everything we did together, do you really think that I could have another woman? Dammit, what sort of man do you think I am?'

She sat eaten up with misery, her narrow shoulders slumped as she stared at Romeo's ears.

After what she'd overheard in the hotel, what was she supposed to think?

'OK.' He calmed down and tried another approach. 'We both got more than a little carried away last night, Joanna, but did you hear what I said to you while we were making love? I said I loved you. Do you remember that?'

Her face flamed and she nodded slowly.

Of course she remembered. Those words were branded on her heart and in her memory.

'And do you think I said those words lightly?'

She held back the tears. 'I think men say a lot of things they don't mean to get a woman into bed.'

'But you were already in my bed,' Seb reminded her quietly. 'I told you that I loved you *after* we'd already committed ourselves to making love. Remember that, Joanna. I had no reason to say those words. No reason except that I wanted to say them. And I wanted to say them because I meant them. And what I want to know now is why you didn't believe me. Why did you run, Joanna? Was it the papers?'

'No.' She shook her head, totally confused by what he was saying. None of it made sense. 'I admit I was upset at first and it'll give me problems with Alice James for weeks to come, but it wasn't the papers that made me leave.'

'What, then?' His voice was urgent and she lifted her eyes to his, knowing that she had to confront him about what she'd heard.

'Because of Gabby. Because I can't share you with Gabby.'

'Gabby?' He stared at her, a stunned expression on his handsome face. 'What has Gabby to do with anything?'

'I heard you, Seb.' A salty tear trickled, unchecked, down her cheek. 'I heard you talking to her.'

'Talking—?' He broke off and understanding dawned. 'And what exactly did you overhear, Joanna? What did I say?'

'That I wasn't going to make a difference to anything,' she said flatly, wondering why she had to remind him of his own conversation. 'That nothing needed to change between you two just because I was on the scene.'

Seb gave a groan and rubbed a hand over his stubbled jawline. 'No wonder you were upset. I had no idea you'd heard that conversation. I'm sorry, Joanna.'

'What for?' She tried to keep her voice steady. 'For the fact that I overheard or the fact that you dismissed me so readily?'

'No.' He shook his head and his voice rang with sincerity. 'It isn't what you think, although I can't blame you for thinking it. I just wish you'd confronted me in the hotel and then we could have avoided this confusion. I wish you'd trusted me, Joanna.'

Why should she? She'd never been given any reason to trust anyone before.

'Gabby—'

'Gabby is nothing to do with us.' His jaw clenched and he breathed out heavily. 'Gabby is business, Joanna. Business that I don't often talk about. But I should have talked about it with you. I see that now. I was foolish not to.'

She looked at him warily, desperately wanting to believe him but unable to expose herself to the possibility of more hurt. More disappointment.

'Business?'

'Yes, business.' He gave a long sigh. 'Look, there are some things I need to tell you. Things I probably should have told you a while ago.'

'What?'

Seb was silent for a moment and the expression was suddenly bleak. 'You asked me once about my family,' he said finally, staring across the moor and not meeting her eyes.

'And you told me about your brother and sister who run the business,' she said, nodding as she recalled his words.

'That's right…' He hesitated and then took a deep breath. 'But I didn't tell you about my other sister. My little sister.'

Her eyes widened. 'You have another sister?'

'Had.' He corrected her in a quiet voice. 'I had another sister. She died when I was twelve.'

'Oh, Seb…' Instinctively Joanna reached out a hand and rested it on his arm. 'What happened?'

'She had a congenital heart condition so she was always breathless and blue around the lips, but she managed to lead a happy life. Then they decided that they needed to correct the defect so they operated.'

Joanna's hand tightened on his arm. 'Did she die?'

'No. Well, not because of the heart defect.' He shook his head. 'The oxygen supply became disconnected during the operation and the anaesthetist didn't notice. As a result she was left severely brain damaged and disabled.'

Joanna closed her eyes. 'Oh, no…'

'It almost wrecked our family,' Seb told her in a quiet voice. 'My parents blamed themselves for letting her have the operation, but that was ridiculous, of course, because Kate would have died without it. But the strain of caring for a severely disabled child on a daily basis put pressure on everyone.'

'It must have been dreadful.'

'Well, we were luckier than some because at least we had money.' Seb gave a short laugh. 'It didn't bring my sister back and it didn't get rid of the pain we all felt, but it did help with practical things and that means quite a lot when you're caring for a child twenty-four hours a day. That was when I realised that I wanted to be a doctor.' He paused and looked at Joanna for the first time. 'It was also when I realised what I wanted to do with my money.'

'You mean use it to support yourself while you worked with disabled children?'

He hesitated. 'Not entirely. I wasn't very old when Kate had her accident but even so I was aware of the sort of pressure that having a child with a disability was putting on the family. It's very hard to have anything approaching a normal life because everything revolves around the child. Some families never get away from it. I wanted to help those families.'

Joanna's heart beat faster as she waited to hear what he had to say. 'So what did you do?'

Seb gathered up the reins and gave a tired smile. 'Let's go home now and I'll show you.'

Seb drove for half an hour and then turned down a private driveway lined with trees that led to a beautiful old house. There were no signs, nothing to indicate it was anything other than a private residence.

'Seb?' Joanna turned to him, puzzled. 'What is this place?'

'Wait and see.' Seb parked the car and Joanna followed him up the steps to the front door.

He pressed the bell and waited, his broad shoulders tensing slightly as the door opened.

A woman in her early fifties stood in the doorway, her face brightening when she recognised Seb.

'Seb!' A smile spread across her face and she stood back to let them in. 'We weren't expecting you.'

'I know that, but I wanted to introduce you to someone.' Seb turned and took Joanna by the hand, pulling her gently so that she was standing next to him. 'I want you to meet Joanna. Joanna, this is Gabby.'

Joanna gaped at the lady in front of her. This was Gabby? She'd been expecting a blonde dolly bird but instead she was looking at a mature, sensible woman with kind eyes and a very understanding smile.

'I'm very pleased to meet you, dear,' she said warmly, extending a hand which Joanna immediately took. 'I expect you've come to look around.'

Joanna glanced at Seb and he nodded. 'Yes. If that's OK.'

Gabby laughed. 'Isn't that typical of him? This place is his baby—he came up with the idea, he found the property, he chose the staff and he funds the whole thing—but he still asks my permission to look round.'

'It's *our* baby, Gabby,' Seb reminded her gruffly, clearly embarrassed by the eulogy. 'As much yours as mine.'

Joanna couldn't stop staring. 'This place is *yours*?'

'Well, not exactly…' He looked self-conscious and distinctly uncomfortable. 'I like to think the children own it really.'

'Children?'

Gabby gave a smile. 'Come and see.'

She led them through the spacious, welcoming hallway into a huge playroom stacked with toys. Several children were playing, ably assisted by two smiling girls.

The girls glanced up when they realised that they had visitors. 'Hello, Seb,' they chorused happily, and he grinned at them.

'Afternoon, Katrin—Helena. All well?'

Katrin? Helena?

Weren't they two of the women who'd rung Seb? Women she'd assumed were girlfriends?

Gabby moved closer to Joanna.

'As you've probably gathered, we're basically a sanctuary where parents can bring their children when they need a rest. Caring for a child with a disability can be physically and mentally exhausting, and families benefit no end from being able to have a break. That's what we give them.' Gabby gave a quiet smile. 'We take them for a week, sometimes longer, and sometimes the parents stay, too. Thanks to Seb, we have a fantastically skilled team of staff who can deal with medical, social and emotional problems.'

So this was why he was always speaking to Gabby. Joanna closed her eyes. Once again she'd misjudged the man. It was becoming a habit.

Gabby was talking again. 'We have a staff ratio of two to one. Sometimes one to one if that's what we think the family needs. Come and see the rest of the house.'

Joanna was silent as they toured the pretty bedrooms, decorated in various styles designed to appeal to children. She was shown the dining room, the garden with its beautiful brightly coloured play area and a huge swimming pool complex.

'Obviously for some of our guests who are more physically disabled, the pool is wonderful therapy,' Gabby told her as they stopped at the poolside. 'We have specially trained physiotherapists who come and help us.'

'It's fantastic…' Joanna's voice was little more than a croak as she turned to Seb. 'But you're away working all the time. How involved are you?'

Gabby laughed. 'He lets us use his money!' Then her smile faded and her eyes softened with affection as they rested on Seb. 'And he's very involved. He knows most of the children who come here and we often discuss cases with him. But obviously he's not involved on a day-to-day basis. That's what he employs me for. Anyway, I've talked enough and I'm sure you two want some time on your own so I'll leave you in peace. I'll be in the gym if you need me—Daniel is having some physio this afternoon and I want to see how he's getting on.'

With that she walked down the corridor, leaving them alone together.

'I've done it again, haven't I?' Joanna felt totally mortified. 'I've jumped to conclusions. I feel such a fool. I didn't know about Gabby—'

'You're not a fool,' Seb said roughly, taking her by the arms and turning her to face him. 'If anyone's a fool here, it's me. I should have realised what you'd be thinking. The girls are always calling me, telling me how particular children are doing. I should have realised how it would look to you.'

He hadn't been chatting to girlfriends. He'd been talking with other staff about his little patients.

Joanna shook her head slowly. 'I'm sorry.'

'Don't be. There's just one thing that worries me, and it's the same thing that worried Gabby.' His eyes were intent on hers. 'Will you expect me to give this place up?'

Joanna's eyes widened. 'What?'

'It's a big part of my life,' he confessed, 'financially and emotionally. I could understand if my wife thought it was too big a commitment—'

Wife?

She blinked, wondering if she'd heard Seb correctly. 'You haven't got a wife.' Her voice was barely a whisper and a slow smile spread across his face.

'Not yet, but I'm working on it.' He cupped her face in his hands and stared into her eyes. 'Joanna Weston, will you take me to be your lawfully wedded husband, together with all my assets which include responsibility for the welfare and happiness of at least eighty children…?'

Joanna stared at him in stunned silence and then finally found her voice. 'Are you asking me to marry you?'

He nodded.

'But—'

'And it's probably only fair to warn you straight away that I can't take no for an answer.' His sexy blue eyes twinkled as he looked at her. 'I bumped into Alice James on my way to find you earlier, and she had few things to say to me…'

Joanna groaned and covered her eyes with her hand. 'You don't have to tell me. I can imagine.'

'I'm sure you can.' He removed her hands gently and a wicked smile crossed his face. 'So are you going to silence the gossips and marry me, or shock the village and live in wild, abandoned sin? Which do you prefer?'

Marry him? Was he really asking her to marry him?

'Seb…' Joanna licked dry lips and he groaned as his gaze followed her movement.

'Don't do that—please! It reminds me too much of wild, abandoned sin. There's only so much a man can stand and we're in a public building. Say you'll marry me.'

'I don't know, Seb.'

His smile faded. 'Why not? Is it because of all this?' He gestured around the house and his broad shoulders sagged slightly. 'That was what Gabby was afraid of. She thought that any woman I married might find this too much of a responsibility and want me to give it up.'

Joanna shook her head. 'It isn't anything to do with the house. What you do here is wonderful, Seb, and it's part of who you are. You're the most generous man I've ever met and if I were your wife I'd never expect you to give it up.'

'If? Could you do better than if?' His voice was hoarse. 'Could you put me out of my misery and say yes?'

'But how would it work, Seb? You travel around the world, doing your work. You never stay in one place—'

'Because I never had a reason to. Until now.' He lifted a hand and stroked a strand of blonde hair away from her eyes. 'Believe me, sweetheart, I wouldn't have any trouble staying in one place if you were there with me.'

Her heart turned over. 'You mean it? You'd stay here?'

He smiled and cupped her face in his hands. 'Of course. Did you think I was planning to travel the world and leave you behind?'

'I don't know what I thought.' She looked at him anxiously. 'I just can't see you as a GP for ever.'

'How well you know me.' Seb gave a wry smile and a shrug. 'You're right about that. I couldn't be a GP for ever. But it's time I got more involved with the running of this place. I've always wanted to but it's never been the right time.' He stroked her cheek with his hand, his expression serious. 'Maybe now is the right time. We can buy a house and you can carry on working at the practice until…' He broke off and she lifted an eyebrow.

'Until what?'

He was strangely hesitant. 'Until you're ready to have our babies. I'm sorry you lost your other child, Joanna, and I know you'll never forget it.'

Her stomach flipped at his words. *Seb's babies.* She hadn't even thought about it before. Hadn't dare think about it.

'So what do you say, Joanna?' He took a deep breath

and his eyes searched hers. 'Will you marry me, sweet-heart?'

'Yes.' She said the word softly and a smile spread across her face. 'Oh, yes. I certainly will.'

He gave a long sigh and closed his eyes. 'Thank God. For a minute there you had me seriously worried.' He opened his eyes again and pulled her closer. 'And what about the babies bit? Is it a yes to that, too?'

She nodded, strangely shy. 'Yes. I love you, Seb. There's nothing I want more than to marry you if you're sure you want me. And have your babies.'

'If I'm sure.' He stared down at her and a smile spread across his face. 'Oh, I'm sure. Very sure. And there's something we've got to do quickly.'

'What?' Joanna started to laugh as he all but dragged her back to the car. 'Where are we going?'

'To see Doris Parker.'

'Doris?' She looked at him in astonishment. 'Doris Parker in the newsagent's? Why?'

'Because, my love, I want the whole world to know that I love you and she's the quickest way I know of spreading news.' He turned to her with a broad grin. 'One word to Doris and within minutes everyone in the village will know that I'm going to marry you.'

Joanna started to laugh, knowing that he was right. 'And you're happy to settle down here? Knowing that your life will never be private again?'

He nodded and touched her cheek, his expression suddenly serious. 'I don't care where I live as long as it's with you, and I don't care what people say about me as long as you're by my side.'

By his side.

Tears filled her eyes and she leaned forward to kiss him. 'That's exactly where I'm going to be, Seb. By your side. For ever. Let's go and tell Doris.'

Modern Romance™
...seduction and
passion guaranteed

Tender Romance™
...love affairs that
last a lifetime

Sensual Romance™
...sassy, sexy and
seductive

Blaze
...sultry days and
steamy nights

Medical Romance™
...medical drama on
the pulse

Historical Romance™
...rich, vivid and
passionate

27 new titles every month.

*With all kinds of Romance for
every kind of mood...*

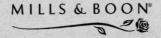

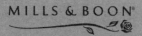

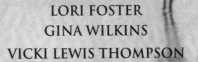

MILLS & BOON
FOREIGN AFFAIRS
A captivating 12 book collection of sun-kissed seductions.
Enjoy romance around the world.
DON'T MISS BOOK 10
caribbean caress–
Indulgence in the sun...
Available from 5th July
Available at most branches of WH Smith, Tesco, Martins, Borders, Eason, Sainsbury's and most good paperback bookshops.
FA/RTL/10

FREE

2 BOOKS
AND A SURPRISE GIFT!

We would like to take this opportunity to thank you for reading this Mills & Boon® book by offering you the chance to take TWO more specially selected titles from the Medical Romance™ series absolutely FREE! We're also making this offer to introduce you to the benefits of the Reader Service™—

★ FREE home delivery   ★ FREE gifts and competitions
★ FREE monthly Newsletter   ★ Exclusive Reader Service discount
★ Books available before they're in the shops

Accepting these FREE books and gift places you under no obligation to buy; you may cancel at any time, even after receiving your free shipment. Simply complete your details below and return the entire page to the address below. **You don't even need a stamp!**

YES! Please send me 2 free Medical Romance books and a surprise gift. I understand that unless you hear from me, I will receive 4 superb new titles every month for just £2.55 each, postage and packing free. I am under no obligation to purchase any books and may cancel my subscription at any time. The free books and gift will be mine to keep in any case.

M2ZEC

Ms/Mrs/Miss/Mr ....Initials ....
BLOCK CAPITALS PLEASE
Surname ....
Address ....
....
....Postcode ....

Send this whole page to:
UK: FREEPOST CN81, Croydon, CR9 3WZ
EIRE: PO Box 4546, Kilcock, County Kildare (stamp required)

Offer valid in UK and Eire only and not available to current Reader Service subscribers to this series. We reserve the right to refuse an application and applicants must be aged 18 years or over. Only one application per household. Terms and prices subject to change without notice. Offer expires 30th September 2002. As a result of this application, you may receive offers from other carefully selected companies. If you would prefer not to share in this opportunity please write to The Data Manager at the address above.

Mills & Boon® is a registered trademark owned by Harlequin Mills & Boon Limited.
Medical Romance™ is being used as a trademark.